One Step Ahead of the

POSSE

Walt Coburn

THORNDIKE
CHIVERS

This Large Print edition is published by Thorndike Press®, Waterville, Maine USA and by BBC Audiobooks, Ltd, Bath, England.

Published in 2005 in the U.S. by arrangement with Golden West Literary Agency.

Published in 2005 in the U.K. by arrangement with Golden West Literary Agency.

U.S. Hardcover 0-7862-7796-3 (Western)
U.K. Hardcover 1-4056-3478-2 (Chivers Large Print)
U.K. Softcover 1-4056-3479-0 (Camden Large Print)

The text of this Large Print edition is unabridged.
Other aspects of the book may vary from the original edition.

Set in 16 pt. Plantin by Minnie B. Raven.

Printed in the United States on permanent paper.

British Library Cataloguing-in-Publication Data available

Library of Congress Cataloging-in-Publication Data

Coburn, Walt, 1889–1971.
    One step ahead of the posse / by Walt Coburn.
      p. cm. — (Thorndike press large print Western)
    ISBN 0-7862-7796-3 (lg. print : hc : alk. paper)
    1. Large type books.   2. Western stories. gsafd I. Title.
II. Thorndike Press large print Western series.
PS3505.O153O54 2005
813′.52—dc22   2005009874

One Step Ahead

of the

POSSE

One Step Ahead
of the
POSSE

Cast of Characters

BOONE
Honesty was his policy, but it was no life insurance.

JAWBONE SMITH
Drunk or sober he was an ornery coyote.

JUDGE LEE
He killed a man in a duel, but the battle with his conscience went on.

JEREMY LEE
He had gambling blood, and was ready to spill it to keep the odds on his side.

TEX HARMER
He was a town marshal who kept the town under control — for his own benefit.

BEAVER BROWN
His need for revenge made him angry enough to drive a man mad!

Chapter 1

Jawbone Strikes

The boy Boone must have been about nineteen years old when he learned for sure that Jawbone Smith was not his father. Jawbone was getting over one of his big drunks and let it slip when he was scared he was dying. And later, when Jawbone come out of it and sat around the cabin drinking black coffee spiked with corn whisky, he kept watching Boone out of the ends of his bloodshot eyes. Boone knew he was remembering that he'd said Boone wasn't his own child. And after the boy had fixed him up some cold tomatoes, Jawbone came out with what was on his mind.

"I recollect a-tellin' you that I wa'n't yore paw. I reckon you'll be a-runnin' off from me one of these days when I kain't watch you."

Boone told Jawbone that it didn't make no difference either one way or the other, and that he didn't aim to quit Jawbone. There wasn't much sense in runnin' off because where would he run to, anyhow? And with Jawbone down with rheumatism, he'd be a skunk to quit him.

That tickled Jawbone and the ugly look went out of his eyes. Boone stayed on with him.

They started up the Chisholm Trail with the SL herd that spring. Jawbone made a dicker for a secondhand outfit for Boone. And the trail boss, who took to the boy right off, put him on as horse wrangler. Boone had been up the trail twice before and knew the country from the Llano Etacada all the way to Miles City. Jawbone had always taught him to keep his eyes open and his mouth shut. He had ways of punishing Boone when the boy couldn't remember a landmark or a brand on a horse or cow-brute. Ways that cut like a knife into the sensitive heart of the youngster.

Like the time when Boone couldn't recollect where he'd seen a certain sorrel gelding with a blotched brand on its thigh. Jawbone made him ride into town wearing a calico sunbonnet he'd picked up somewhere, and no doubt saved for just that purpose. And while Jawbone was in the saloon getting drunk, Boone had to stay outside and hold the horses. The men that passed made coarse remarks, till Boone's face was as hot as if he stood over a stove. Then a crowd of town boys gathered and poked fun at him. White-lipped, trembling like he was took down with chills and fever, Boone stood their taunts.

Boone had never had a chance to play with other boys. He'd hardly ever even spoke to another boy. Jawbone forbade it, for one thing, and then they never stayed in town. They were always on the trail. Now as the group of boys gathered, Boone ignored them, or made out to ignore them. Some ways, he hated town kids with their smart tongues and their town clothes. But behind that hatred was a pitiful sort of wistfulness. He sensed that he was missing his boyhood — the games and the laughter, and the comradeship.

Boone had sat his horse, his face white now under the flopping sunbonnet. Then one of the older boys picked up a stick and hit Boone's horse. The next instant that boy was down in the dirt there by the hitch rack and the sunbonneted Boone, half his size, was biting and gouging and kicking him. Cursing like a bullwhacker, sobbing in his anger, he was driving hard, toil-toughened fists into the other boy's face with a ferocity of purpose that was almost maniacal. When Jawbone pushed through the drunken, cheering mob and pried Boone's fingers from the older lad's throat, the beaten town boy was unconscious. Jawbone threw Boone up on his horse and they quit town in a hurry. Back in the dirt of the street, stained and torn, lay the sunbonnet.

Boone was still shaking and sobbing. And that night, at their lonely camp, the boy was too sick from reaction to eat. Jawbone let him alone, but now and then he eyed him with a peculiar expression.

And some time later on, when they stayed with a bunch of bearded, hard-eyed men in the Mogollones, Boone heard Jawbone telling these men about the sunbonnet fight.

"The young un's a killer, mark what I say! If any of you stay unhung that long, you'll see him make a name for hisse'f."

That was about a year before they started up with the SL herd and Boone saw his first real gun fight. It happened in a saloon in Abilene. Jawbone had set Boone at an empty poker table in a far corner and told him to stay there. And in spite of the invitations from the cowboys to go up the street and visit the stores and see the town, Boone had stuck to his corner, mostly unnoticed. Jawbone was leaning against the bar, drinking too much, and getting more close-mouthed with each drink. That was Jawbone's way.

Boone watched him with a sort of mingled pity and loathing. He was hoping Jawbone wouldn't come down with the snakes again, and holler and groan and carry on disgraceful. Because if he done so, Till Driscoll, the trail boss, would pay him off. And Boone liked Driscoll and the SL cowboys more than he liked most of Jawbone's strange companions of the twisted trails they travelled, mostly alone.

Now, Boone suddenly straightened in his chair. He seen Jawbone drop his right hand on his gun. The next moment Jawbone and a tall cow-puncher faced one another. The roar of their guns filled the saloon. The tall cowboy's knees sagged, and he pitched sidewise on to the floor. Jawbone pushed through the crowd and outside. Nobody made a move to stop him. Boone was about to follow when an SL cowboy noticed him.

"You stay here, boy." His voice was gruff but not unkind. Some other cowboys were laying the wounded man on a table. Boone reckoned the man was dying. He was talking, but the boy was too far away to catch the words. Then there was a sort of moaning sigh. Then somebody covered the man on the table with a tarp, and Boone knew he'd died.

The crowd, all but a little knot of cow-hands that Boone took to be the dead man's friends, moved back to their drinks and their cards. The fiddle and accordion began playing once more as if nothing had happened. The swamper was throwing dirt on the dark pool there in front of the bar. Now they carried out the tarp-wrapped body.

Boone sat there, sort of numb in his bewilderment, until, after a spell, the same SL cowboy came back to where he sat and handed him a drink of whisky.

"Throw that into you, boy. You look peaked, and no wonder. This ain't any fit place for a kid like you to be."

Boone drank the whisky. It was the first time he'd ever tasted it. Jawbone had never offered him a drink and Boone had never asked for any of the stuff that made men act loco. He choked over the raw liquor, and the cowboy grinned.

"When that warms you through, you'n me will go on to camp. Till says yo're goin' on with us. I reckon that's the last you'll see of that old man of yourn. And a good riddance. He's a bad un. And Bob Harmer's boys will give him a hot chase. That's their herd a-comin' behind us. Yep, I reckon that's the last you'll see of yore paw."

It was on the tip of the boy's tongue to tell the cowboy that Jawbone was not his father. But the long habit of keeping his mouth shut held back the words. That slug of whisky was warming him up. He felt a little light-headed when they rode out of town to the SL camp. He kept wondering why Jawbone had killed Bob Harmer, one of the three Harmer brothers who owned the Y Down iron.

When the boys came trickling into camp that evening, more than one fetched Boone some sort of present. Candy, and clothing, and a bright neck-scarf, and a pair of spurs. Till Driscoll asked him, in a sort of fatherly way, if he had any other kinfolks. Boone said he didn't know of any.

"Then we'll kinda ride herd on you, Boone. And the sooner you forget Jawbone, the better for you."

"I ain't a-grievin'," said Boone quietly, "I was just thinkin' some."

He corralled his horses, and the night hawk took the remuda over. After supper, Boone rolled in between his blankets. He

15

could hear the murmur of voices around the camp-fire and reckoned they were talking over the killing. Sleep would not come, somehow. He lay there, trying to count the big stars.

About first guard time, some men rode into camp. Boone saw the glitter of their guns by the firelight. They were after Jawbone. Boone was glad they hadn't caught him yet. Jawbone had beat him and treated him ornery a lot of times, but Boone couldn't help but look back and remember the other times when they camped alone and Jawbone would talk far into the night of things that interested him. Things like the war between the North and South, of Indian fights, and trips into Mexico on cattle raids. Tales of Quantrell and the James boys, whom Jawbone seemed to know. Stories about Kit Carson, and Bowie, and Pauline Weaver, and Jim Bridger. The story of the Alamo, so deeply planted in the heart of every Texan. Of the fierce battle of Adobe Walls. Of steamboats that went up the river from St. Louis. Jawbone liked to talk about things like that, when he wasn't drunk.

Boone's eyes ached and there was a big lump in his throat. He felt sort of lost and bewildered. He almost wished he'd followed Jawbone. He knew where Jawbone would be heading for. Once, a couple of years before, Jawbone had taken the boy there. Till Driscoll and one of the strangers quit the fire and came over to where Boone had unrolled his bed.

"Asleep, son?"

"No, sir."

"I was wonderin' if you had any idea where Jawbone would be headed for." The trail boss spoke in a kindly way.

Boone sat up in bed, a tightness to his lips that made him look more like a man than a boy.

"Jawbone," he said simply, "has fed me and give me clothes and a bed. Don't you reckon I'd be purty much of a skunk if I was to put men on his trail?"

The men looked at him in silence. Then Driscoll spoke.

"I reckon yo're about right, son. Yes, sir, I reckon you're right." He took the stranger back to the fire.

Chapter 2

Gratitude

But Boone had not seen the last of Jawbone. One night, three weeks later, as he slept, a heavy hand was laid on his mouth. Jawbone's whisper filled his ear. There was the odor of whisky.

"Roll out, young un. Don't make no noise. Meet me in that coulee behind the bed wagon. Come quiet, mind, or I'll beat the hide off yore back!"

Boone carried his boots and his little muslin warsack in his hands. He found Jawbone in the coulee with two saddled horses. They rode away in silence, avoiding the remuda and the bedded herd where a cowboy sang the lonesome tune of the "Lament" to the star-filled sky.

The horse under Boone was a splendid animal. The stirrups were too long and Boone shoved his feet in the stirrup leathers. Not until the camp was far behind them did Jawbone break the silence.

"I come for you quick as I could. The

boys has bin houndin' me clost. But ol' Jawbone was too slick for 'em. Too slick. But they gimme a deal, young un. They did, for a fact. And I dealt 'em some hot lead that cooled 'em down. Did you miss me any?"

"I reckon I did," admitted the boy, "but they was almighty good to me, and Till Driscoll 'lowed that when we got back to the Rio Hondo he'd get me a home with some folks that'd take him in."

"What in heck need have you got for a home? Splittin' wood and haulin' water for wimmenfolks. Feedin' hawgs and learnin' Sunday school papers. That's no life for a young un as has bin from Mexico to Canada and back twict, while there's white-headed men down there as 'ud be lost if they stepped outa their own barn-yard. If it's a plough you'd care to foller, then go back and get 'prenticed out to some mossback farmer. But if you got a hankerin' for to see life, trail with Jawbone Smith and I'll show you things as'll make yore eyes pop. Yo're growin' up fast. Big for yore age and wiser'n a lot of men. And ol' Jawbone ain't forgittin' what you told Till Driscoll and Rance Harmer. That you wouldn't tell where I'd gone. And you knowed, too. I got the yarn from a feller as heard it at Abilene. You done right by me, young un. I ain't forgettin'. And here's the proof."

He handed Boone a filled cartridge belt and a holstered gun. He'd never allowed the boy to own a gun, though he'd spent many an hour teaching him to shoot. Boone's eyes lighted up with pleasure. The belt was much too large, and Jawbone took his knife and cut it down to fit. The heavy gun sagged down on the slim waist. Boone's hand stroke its cedar handle with an affectionate touch. He had all a boy's longing for guns. He felt proud and manly. And the feel of that horse between his slim legs was a thing beyond words. The best horse Boone had ever ridden, though Jawbone never kept any but the best he could trade for or steal.

They rode all night long and part of the next morning. Sometimes, Boone would doze off in the saddle, his half-sleep filled with strange dreams. He was mighty glad when Jawbone led the way up into a timbered canyon and pointed to a little cabin where three men squatted around a camp fire, eating.

"Here's camp, young un. Unsaddle and hobble these horses!"

"See you got the kid, Jawbone," said one

of the tough-looking trio. "Have any trouble?"

"Nary. Where's the whisky? How'd you boys come out?"

"Tol'able," grinned a lean-jawed man with a shock of hair that screened his eyes, giving him a dog-like appearance. "About fifty head. Them Y Down cowboys will ride short strings the rest of the way up the trail."

There was a skillet half-full of antelope steaks and some beans and bannock bread. Jawbone was already eating when Boone finished hobbling the two horses.

"Tie into the grub," Jawbone told him.

Boone helped himself. There were no plates or knives or forks. The boy was at home in such crude surroundings, and he shovelled beans on to the meat and bread and wolfed the food. But he did not drink any of the coffee that simmered in a blackened pail from which the men drank.

The three men looked at Boone with a brutish curiosity. He returned their stares with a steady gaze. He made no effort to talk to them. He knew them for what they were, horse thieves. Just as Jawbone was a horse thief. Boone hated them and their kind. A cowardly pack, most of them, coyotes following the trail herds. Stealing what

21

they could steal. Running away, dodging the eyes of honest men. Human coyotes.

Boone wished that he was back at the SL camp. It hurt him to contemplate what Till Driscoll and the cowboys would be saying. They were men, and they kept true to a man's code. In most parts of the cow country the law hung horse thieves. Boone hoped that Till Driscoll and the SL boys would kinda understand how he had to foller along with Jawbone. If he was to run off from Jawbone, he'd be follered. And when Jawbone ketched him, there'd be heck to pay all around.

Full of food, Boone crawled into the shade and dozed. Jawbone and the other men were talking in low tones. They were talking about the SL outfit now. Boone fought off the desire to sleep and listened with all his might.

They were planning to raid the SL remuda.

"The button can stay here and look after what stuff we got," said Jawbone. "No need to let him know where we're goin'."

"Supposin' he won't stay?" growled one of the three.

"He'll stay." Jawbone's harsh laugh had an ugly sound. "He knows I'll whip the hide off him if he don't do what I tell him.

But just the same, no use lettin' him know where we're goin'. He thinks a heap of Driscoll. . . . Gimme that jug once more."

Covertly, sleep dispersed now. Boone looked at the group there at the fire. The boy saw how Jawbone had changed since that night at Abilene when he had killed Bob Harmer. The man looked thin, and tired, and old. His bloodshot eyes were slitted and evil, and there were deep lines at the corners of his thin-lipped mouth, bitter, desperately grim lines. Jawbone was now unwrapping a grimy bandage from an unhealed bullet wound in his thigh. He cleansed the wound with whisky against the profane protests of the three. His eyes suddenly silenced them.

"Mebby I'll have to learn ye who's boss here," he snarled at them. "Mind what happened to Andy when he got the idee he was goin' to run things. He got shot."

The three flinched under Jawbone's slitted stare. He cursed the sting of the raw whisky and tied the bandage back over the wound.

"We'll pull out in about three hours," he told them. "Better get some sleep." He stretched out alongside Boone.

Utterly weary, the boy slept fitfully. Nightmare figures rode through his dreams. Jawbone's muttering and snoring kept waking him. He rose when Jawbone did, and washed in the creek. Jawbone was in a surly mood and took no share in the conversation. It was mid-afternoon, and when the four men had cooked and eaten some grub, Jawbone sent Boone along with the long-jawed man to fetch in the horses. There was a makeshift corral, and the horses were held in a box canyon that was ingeniously fenced across a narrow place between the canyon walls. There was good feed and water there and the place was ideal for the lawless calling of the horse thief.

The four men roped out the best among the stolen horses. Besides the Y Down horses, there were about twenty branded Lazy K. Boone knew that the Lazy K herd was coming up the trail behind the Harmer herd.

"Haze these horses back up in the canyon, young un," ordered Jawbone. "Us boys is takin' a little *pasear* over the hills to see what the bear found when he crossed the mountain. You stay at camp. Don't leave, or I'll break yore back!"

Boone made no reply. He drove the horses back up the canyon and roped a stout-looking dun pony from the stolen

24

cavvy. He changed his saddle to the dun, and led his own horse back to the cabin where he hobbled him. Then he rode down the canyon, taking care not to crowd too close behind the horse thieves. Once out of the canyon and on a long ridge spotted with scrub pine, he chose a course that would take him somewhere near where he'd be likely to find the SL outfit. He'd kept track of the course last night, reading direction from the stars and by instinct.

The dun pony was fast and tough. Boone's light weight was in his favor. And he knew how to ride a horse so as to get the most out of the animal.

He reckoned, when sundown came, that he had left the men far behind. He was travelling across the rolling prairie country now. Dusk, then darkness. The dun horse was still travelling at a long, tireless trot. Boone's hip was rubbed raw by the heavy gun he carried, but he didn't mind that.

Now, out of the night ahead, came the song of a cowboy as he rode around the bedded herd. There would be four men on guard.

He slowed his horse down and began singing. His boy's voice, singing "The Dying Cowboy," rose clear and sweet. Now the cowboy on guard ceased his song.

Every man in the SL outfit knew Boone's singing. He'd sung to them many a time in the evenings. They knew that the runaway had returned, that his song was to let them know who was riding up out of the night.

Till Driscoll was the first man the boy found.

"Gosh amighty, young feller, we bin wonderin' what had become of you! Yore saddle and hoss was there tied to the bed wagon. But you was gone. Then we picked up the sign of two horses and we decided yore paw had done showed up like a bad dollar."

"Yes, sir. He come for me." Boone's voice was strained and husky sounding. "He taken me away."

"But you run off from him and come back to the SL. That's the right thing to do! And if he comes here again, he'll get a full dose of lead."

"I got to go back to him," said the boy. "I come to tell you that four fellers is a-comin' to whittle some horses outa the remuda. I come to tell you so's you'd have an extra guard put on."

"That's right white of you, son, and I'm shore obliged. I already got some boys out with the cavvy. One of the Y Down men rode over to camp to-day and told us they'd lost some horses last night. Their night hawk was killed. Clubbed over the head from behind, near as they could tell. Murdered in cold blood." Till Driscoll looked at the chunky dun horse.

"Yo're ridin' a Y Down horse, Boone. I happen to know the dun pony. I ain't askin' you how you come to be forkin' one of the horses that was stole last night. You've rode here to do me a favor. I don't need to ask who's comin' to try to steal some SL horses. When they come, we'll be ready. Now, you better go on to the wagon and go to bed. There's no law of man or of God that says you have to go trailin' with a horse thief like Jawbone Smith, even if he is yore paw."

"I bin thinkin' 'er all out," said Boone quietly. "I thought 'er out before I started for here. I'm goin' with Jawbone. Leastways, for a spell. This is the first time I ever hollered on him or on any man. I hope I never have to do it again, because it makes a feller feel almighty cheap and ornery and low-down. But you'd bin good to me and I don't aim to let you get the worst of it. I'm glad I come, but I can't make out to stay, Mister Driscoll. If Jawbone gets killed, then I'll come back, I'd hate to have him get killed tonight, but that ain't for me to decide. I know I ain't bound by no law to trail with him. It's just somethin' inside of me that says it's the thing to do."

Till Driscoll was reminded of a picture he had once seen of a drunkard and his dog, a little, underfed dog that remained loyal in spite of abuse. Something of that same loyalty was prompting Boone to do as he was doing. Its bigness awed the trail boss a little.

"I reckon, son, it's up to you to decide. Some ways, you're a growed-up man. You do like you feel you had ought to do. But whatever you do, or wherever you go, remember Till Driscoll is yore friend and if ever you need a friend, hunt me up. So long, Boone. Good luck! Just keep on thinkin' things out and you'll be a real man."

"I aim to be," said Boone quietly. "I don't want to be a danged horse thief."

"I'm blessed," said the cowman, "if I see how a man like Jawbone can be father of a young un like you."

"He ain't my father. I don't reckon he's even any kind of kinfolks. So long, sir."

And before Till Driscoll could recover from his astonishment, Boone had ridden away into the night.

Chapter 3

Courage

It was past sunrise when Boone reached the horse thief camp in the box canyon. He unsaddled the dun horse and turned him in with the other horses. Then he made a fire and cooked some meat and bannock bread. He kept thinking of what he had done and wondering what had happened. He looked up, startled, to see Jawbone riding up the canyon alone.

Jawbone looked haggard, and his skin showed a grayish pallor. His left shirt sleeve was soggy with red from shoulder to wrist. The arm dangled limply at his side. He dismounted stiffly and made for the jug. He drank the fiery stuff as if it was water as he sat cross-legged on the ground. His horse was sweat-streaked and played out.

Boone eyed the man in silence. He knew better than to ask a question or volunteer a remark. Jawbone's thin-lipped mouth twitched into a twisted smile.

"Well, young un, we shore made a losin'. Fetch some water and cut off this shirt. Quit gapin' and get to work." He worked his stiff fingers slowly. "Bone ain't broke. Just through the meat, that's all."

He tilted the jug across his good arm and drank heavily. Then Boone cut away shirt and undershirt and dressed the ugly wound. Jawbone made him bathe the wound with whisky and never even whimpered when the alcohol bit into the raw flesh. Whatever else he might be, the man had courage of a sort.

"Now go wrangle the horses, young un," he said, when Boone wrapped a bandage made of a new shirt that Till Driscoll had given him. "We gotta be rattlin' our hocks. Them boys might be a-follerin' closer than I figger. Gosh, they give us a hot welcome! The other boys drawed quick tickets to Hades. Get them horses, dang it!"

Boone wrangled the horses and threw them into the corral. Jawbone stood there, sizing them up to pick a good mount. Suddenly, with a muttered curse, he pointed to the chunky dun pony.

"That horse was rode last night. He's sweat marked. Dang yore sneakin' little hide, where was you last night?"

White-lipped, Boone faced the infuriated

30

horse thief. The boy's eyes, gray, flecked with black specks, were unafraid.

"I rode to the SL camp and told Till Driscoll that his remuda was gonna get raided." Boone's voice shook a little.

A whining, snarling sound came from Jawbone's twisted mouth. He picked up a rawhide reata that lay on the ground.

"Peel off yore shirt, you little sneak! I'll learn you a lesson that you'll take to yore grave. Peel that shirt!"

Boone took a couple of steps backward. His right hand moved with lightning speed. His face, white under its tan, was set and grim. He thumbed back the hammer of the big Colt gun. Its long barrel was steady as it pointed at the man.

"Come at me, and so help me heaven, I'll kill you! Yo're done a-whippin' me. Lay a hand on me again and I'll kill you, Jawbone!"

Boone's voice was gritty, harsh. His eyes were cold, and hard, and deadly. Jawbone backed away, a shocked fright stamped on his face, as if he were looking at something that he had seen before — something that chilled his spine.

"If you wa'n't hurt, Jawbone," said Boone, in that same voice that was all the more terrible because the speaker was a mere boy, "I'd quit you here and now. But I'll stay with you till yo're well or a dead one! But don't ever lay a hand on me again. Ever! Because I'll kill you. Do you understand?"

Jawbone nodded. Then he turned away and walked, limping, back to the fire. He sat down on the ground, staring unseeingly into space. Boone took the hobbles off the splendid bay horse he had ridden away from the SL camp and saddled the animal. He swung up into the saddle and rode over to where Jawbone sat.

"Stay here till I get back, Jawbone. Or else go yore way alone. I'm talkin' these stolen horses to the SL camp. Then I'm a-comin' back. I'll come back alone. If yore gone, then I'll go back to the SL outfit. If yo're still here, I'll stay with you and help you."

If Jawbone heard, he gave no sign. He sat like a man whose brain has gone suddenly numb, staring with bloodshot, unwinking eyes at the ground. He was still sitting like that when Boone drove the bunch of stolen horses down the canyon.

Chapter 4

Freedom

It was long after dark when Boone rode back to the camp in the canyon. In his heart, he almost hoped that Jawbone would be gone. But, on the other hand, he was a little relieved to find him sitting squat-legged beside the camp fire, his jug beside him. Boone likened him to an old wolf, crippled and at the mercy of a hound pack.

Jawbone gave him no sort of welcome. He barely glanced up as the boy unsaddled and hobbled his horse, then came over to the fire. Boone sat down across the fire from the man. Neither spoke. Boone ate some cold meat and washed it down with creek water.

He had met some cowboys from the SL and Y Down outfits and had turned over the horses to them.

"All I ask is that you don't foller me," he told them. "Jawbone is hurt bad. I reckon that mebby he'll die. He won't be botherin' you ever again."

They had let him ride away. And he had come back to take care of the man who had raised him.

When he had finished eating, he rolled out a bed for Jawbone and put some big chunks on the fire. Then, without a word, he took a blanket and went away into the darkness.

He knew that, from now on, his back would never be turned to the renegade. Nor would Jawbone ever know where he spread his blankets. Jawbone had lost that intangible thing that separates the sane from the insane. He would kill the boy if the chance came right because he had suddenly become strangely afraid of Boone.

This marked the beginning of a strange partnership. Boone nursed the man until his wounds were healed. When the jug was empty, and when Jawbone had dug up another one and drunk it up, there was no more except a quart that Boone had hid out to nurse him on through his usual case of delirium tremens. Jawbone stayed sober for two months. Ugly of temper, with never a word of thanks to the boy, the man moped around camp like some restless animal penned. Days on end, no word passed between the two.

When grub ran low, Boone would ride into town. Jawbone dared not show his face there because the new town marshal was a cousin to the Harmer boys.

Always, when Boone returned, he hoped to find this half-mad, surly-tempered man gone. Because he feared that some night Jawbone would find his bed ground and one or both of them would be killed. The man brooded about their quarrel. He hated to back down to a boy, even if that boy was a man in build and courage and fighting prowess.

Two months went by while they remained there in the box canyon. Boone, on his several trips to town, had managed to buy some second-hand books from the postmaster. These he read from cover to cover. He had taught himself to write and spell, and whenever he came across a word he did not know, he would write it down on a piece of paper. And the next trip to town he would ask the postmaster the meaning of the word and how to pronounce it. Finally the postmaster gave him a small dictionary, a grammar, and World's History with maps. And so it was that during those two months spent in the box canyon, Boone crowded a half-year's study into his mind. His brain was like an arid sand waste eager to absorb the rain.

With this smattering of knowledge there was slowly born in him a desire to know who he was and something of his family. Cheated of his boyhood, deprived of decent companionship, thrown among thieves and killers of all kinds, he wanted to get into contact with the things he read about in the books.

One night, when Jawbone seemed less surly than usual, and when Boone had, with premeditation, hinted that he might fetch back a jug from town to-morrow, the boy put the question that was uppermost in his mind.

"Jawbone, who am I? Who was my father and mother, and where did you get holt of me?"

Jawbone's lips writhed in a snarl. His eyes glittered in the firelight. Snarling like some animal, his big hands clenching and un-clenching, a thin froth on his twisted lips, the man sat there glaring at him across the fire.

Boone, his hand on his gun, waited for the man to leap at him. But fear held back the renegade. Fear, and the memory of something that writhed in his brain like a poisonous snake.

Now Boone knew that he would never hear the truth from the lips of Jawbone

Smith. He wondered what terrible secret it was that the man held locked in his warped mind. Why did his question bring up such fear, and bitterness, and hatred?

Jawbone got to his feet and stalked away into the night. Boone quit the firelight and slipped into the safety of the blackness. He could hear Jawbone threshing about in the underbrush. Then he heard a hoarse shout, and a few moments later Jawbone came back to the fire lugging a jug he had found hidden. With hands that shook with eagerness, the man pried out the cork and drank like one dying of thirst.

Jawbone got drunk that night. Boone, hidden up on the side of the canyon, could hear the man's muttered curses as he prowled with drunken caution through the brush hunting for him. After half an hour, or perhaps not so long, Jawbone would go back to the fire and his jug. Then he would start out again on his murderous search. But the two months' abstinence had made his system susceptible to the powerful liquor. And before daylight, Jawbone lay there on the ground beside the fire, dead to the world.

At daylight, Boone saddled up and started for town. Jawbone was still unconscious.

At the little cow town, Boone found a knot of men in front of the post office. They were armed, and in the center of the group was the town marshal. They eyed Boone with suspicious eyes. The marshal called him and Boone dismounted and approached the group of grim-faced men.

"Young feller," said the marshal, thumbs hooked in the armholes of his fancy vest, "you bin comin' and goin' for a couple of months. Just where do you come from and where do you go to when you leave town?"

Boone smiled a little. "You ought to know, mister. You've follered me every time."

"And lost yore trail," admitted the marshal grimly. "Yo're as slick as a fox. What's yore game, button?"

"I reckon you know without askin' me. You was with the SL and the Y Down men the night I delivered them stolen horses. You are kinfolks to the Harmers. They agreed not to foller me. You've broke that agreement. You've follered me every time I left town."

The marshal was a small, wiry man with quick eyes that were black as agate. He had coarse black hair, a hawk nose, and his face was badly pock-marked. His mouth was lipless and without a line to show that he had ever smiled. "Tex" Harmer was the killer of the Harmer clan and had quit the Y Down trail herd to take the job of city marshal in the frontier cow town. And Boone knew that he had stayed behind to kill Jawbone because Jawbone had killed Bob Harmer. A gun-thrower, Tex Harmer, and like many another along the cattle trail from Texas, the cow town had been glad to elect a marshal who would shoot first and do his talking later. For these were days when the West was infested with killers, and it took a killer of their own kind to exterminate the breed. And Tex Harmer had come well recommended. He had killed a dozen men or more and was able to sleep at night.

Boone met the glitter of Tex Harmer's black eyes. He figured that the Texan might go for his gun, and he had determined not to be shot down in cold blood. Till Driscoll and the SL boys had told the newly elected marshal that Boone was not a thief or a liar. It stirred up some sort of cold, deadly rancor inside the boy to be falsely questioned now. Because, down in Texas, Tex Harmer was considered but little more than an outlaw, little better than Jawbone Smith.

Harmer turned to the crowd. "This

yearlin' knows aplenty about what happened last night. And I'll get it outa him."

Boone took a step backward. His hand dropped to his gun. The grey eyes that were flecked with tiny black spots narrowed a little, and the boy's lips smiled unpleasantly.

"I've done no wrong. I was at camp last night, and so was Jawbone. Try to lay a-holt of me and I'll shoot."

The grizzled postmaster stepped from the doorway. He pocketed his spectacles and pushed his way into the crowd. Time had been when this white-haired, bent little man had been something of a gun fighter, and his blue eyes blazed like twin sapphire fires.

"Let the lad alone." He placed himself in front of Boone. "Stand back from the boy. There'll be no murder done here."

"There was murder done last night," snapped the marshal. "And a bank robbed. And this boy lives with a horse thief and outlaw. Ask him what he knows about it."

"I don't know anything about any bank robbery or murder," said Boone.

"Prove it," said the marshal, "and I'll believe it — maybe." His black eyes stared at the white-haired old postmaster. "Better

40

keep outa this, Uncle Jake. What's this kid to you?"

"The lad's my friend," said the grizzled old fellow whom every one called Uncle Jake. "And if it's a reputation that you are out after, then pick up the trail of the man that robbed the bank, instead of wasting time bullying a boy that knows nothin' of it. Unless you're scared of catching up with the robbers, you'll do better to be in the saddle than here on the sidewalk."

Tex Harmer's pock-marked face flushed a little. "That'll be all from you, old-timer. Yo're white-headed and old. Otherwise, I'd make you swaller what you said. Now, quit interferin' with the law."

"Law?" snapped Uncle Jake. "What law? Six-shooter law. Lynch law. Tex Harmer's law that lays hand on Tex Harmer's personal enemies and protects Tex Harmer's friends. I know your breed. I'm justice of the peace here in Red Rock. As such, I'll take care of this boy. Take your posse and hit the trail. And while my hair is white and I'm not so limber as I might be, I can still thumb the hammer of the gun I pack. It's a gun that never shot a boy or a man that wasn't given his chance. It's never killed a man from the brush. Can you say as much for your shootin' iron?"

With an impatient oath, Tex Harmer turned away and went down the street to the long hitch rack in front of the saloon. Uncle Jake's blue eyes followed him. Then the old postmaster led Boone inside.

"It's a shame that we must use such men to enforce the law, son. He's no better than the men he hunts."

"He said the bank was robbed, Uncle Jake."

"Yesterday afternoon. Four men rode into town, and while one man held the horses, the other three went inside. They killed the cashier and teller and rode away with what money they could lay hands on."

"Nobody stopped 'em?"

"Tex Harmer wasn't in town. The few men that were here in town were all up at the other end of the street watchin' a horse race that two gamblers had matched. I was there, myself. The bank robbers had a clear field."

"But somebody saw 'em?"

"The swamper at the First and Last Chance. He thought they were four cow-punchers come to town and paid 'em no attention. He's deaf as a post and didn't hear the shootin'. And he was too far away to give any kind of description of the men."

Boone watched Harmer and his posse ride out of town. He was thinking of some tracks he had seen not so far from the trail that led to the box canyon. Tracks of four shod horses crossing a creek. Few men knew those rough bad lands as Boone knew them — every pocket, every look-out point, every cave, and spring, and soap-hole. And he was now almost positive that he could go to the place where the bank robbers were in hiding. But he said nothing to Uncle Jake. After an hour's visit with the old postmaster, Boone purchased his few supplies and rode out of town.

It was a thirty-mile ride back to the box canyon, and the twisting, dodging course that the boy would take would add another ten or fifteen miles to the journey. He knew that Tex Harmer would have him followed. But under the cover of night it would be a simple matter to lose any one who trailed him. What the boy feared most was a bullet in the back as he rode past some brush.

Usually, either going or coming, Boone made a camp in the hills and took two days for the round trip. But a restless uneasiness pushed him now. He'd get Jawbone and quit this country. Things were getting too crowded. It was only a matter of time until the town marshal or some other man located the box canyon.

Boone saw a man on horseback off to the right. He knew that he was being watched through field glasses. He smiled to himself and took a look at the sun. An hour till sunset. He took a course that angled away from the direction of the box canyon and kept to that course until dark. Let 'em watch him! As soon as darkness fell, he swung abruptly to the true course and gave the game-hearted bay its head.

On through the night. Mile after mile. Hour after hour. The bay gelding still at a long trot, stopping now and then, or pulling down to a slower gait. It would take more than an ordinary man to trail him. The night was black but for a quarter moon.

It was still a couple of hours before daylight when Boone rode along the ridges that led to the canyon. He was dozing a little in the saddle.

The sudden crack of a gun brought him awake. He felt the breath of a bullet that droned past his head. Jumping the bay horse aside, he jerked his gun. Some one was shooting at him as he quit the trail and took to the timber. A few moments and Boone was safe. It had been a close call.

Far too close for comfort. He rode now with his gun in his hand. He'd have to get Jawbone out of the canyon before daylight broke. Mebbyso he was too late, even now. Supposin' they'd already found Jawbone? He'd have to risk another ambush, have to get Jawbone away.

The distance to the box canyon was only half an hour's journey, but every foot of the way was nerve-racking and tried Boone's courage. And even when he reached the cabin, he had plenty of reason to expect a bullet from the man he had come to save.

But Jawbone was not there. The ashes of the fire were cold. The supply of grub was gone. No horse grazed there. No saddle lay, covered with its blanket, beside the corral. Jawbone had pulled out.

Boone unsaddled and hobbled his horse. Then he climbed up to one of his hiding places and napped until daylight. He came down and made another search. Half an hour's hunt told him that Jawbone had taken what he wanted and left. And he had not left alone. Four other horses had come there to the cabin and had gone. The empty jug beside the dead camp fire told its mute tale.

Jawbone, renegade, had joined the four

bank robbers. And now Boone knew that it must have been Jawbone, not Tex Harmer or any of his posse, who had ambushed him on the ridge.

With a grim smile, Boone looked at the sunrise. It was the beginning of a new day, the beginning of a new life. Jawbone's six-shooter had ripped away the last tie of loyalty he owed the renegade. From this day on, Boone was free to follow his own way.

"God," he spoke aloud, "I wish that I knowed some prayer words to tell You how I feel! Amen."

Chapter 5

Boone Joins the DHS

Two days later a slim young cowboy rode into a cow camp on the trail from Texas to Montana. His horse was gaunt and leg weary. The finely chiselled face of the boy showed lines of weariness under its dust-coated bronze. But the gray eyes, flicked with black specks, were steady, alight with the sparkle of adventure.

The cow-punchers who were eating supper looked at Boone with a none too friendly eye. Strangers along the cattle trail were more or less under suspicion. A big, broad-shouldered, unshaven man with graying hair looked at him. Boone swung from his saddle and stood outside the circle of men who ate from tin plates.

"Turn yore horse in the cavvy," said the big man, "and help yorself to the grub. You look like you'd come a distance."

"Yes," replied Boone, "I have. And I'm obliged. I can pay for what I eat."

"Nobody asked you to pay, young feller.

This is a cow camp, not a hotel. The DHS don't charge for meals. Fall into it, button, and get the wrinkles outa yore stomach."

There was a kindly twinkle in the trail boss's eyes. He spoke with a soft drawl.

Boone turned his horse into the remuda and filled a plate with bread and meat and beans. The coffee was black and hot and strong. The boy ate hungrily. When he was through, he put his empty plate and cup in the dish pan and picked up a couple of empty buckets. These he filled at the creek and fetched back for the cook. Most of the cowboys, including the trail boss, were catching fresh horses.

Boone began washing the dishes. The cook, a cross-eyed, dour-looking little man with a limp, eyed him with cranky approval.

"Mostly," he said sourly, "these grub-line riders eats and runs without so much as a thankee, go-tuh heck, or how are ye. Hungry stomachs and absent minds. It'd bust their backs to fetch a pail of water or split some wood. I've fed a thousand of 'em."

"Directly I ketch my horse," said Boone, "I'll help you break camp." He went over to the corral.

The trail boss pointed out a roan horse.

"This hoss of yourn looks like he needed a rest. Ride old Pieface. Lookin' for a job?"

"Yes, sir. I'd be proud to hire out. I'll do anything you got to do and try to make a hand at it."

The trail boss nodded. "I'm short-handed. One of my boys got an idee that he was too smart in the head to waste his life punchin' dogies up the trail, so he joins up with some fellers that makes 'er easy. They holds up the Red Rock bank and kills off two pore bank gents that never harmed 'em. A gent named Jawbone Smith rods the deal, so I'm told. And the town marshal of Red Rock, who is a-trailin' 'em, stops at camp last night with a hen-yard posse made up of checker players that'd be dangerous because they're scared plumb green they'll jump Jawbone and these boys.

"A gent named Tex Harmer is the town marshal that's a-ridin' in the lead of this bunch of gun toters. I knowed Tex Harmer before he killed Sam Wallace from behind, and thereby gits a rep as a pistol handler. Yeah, I knowed Tex Harmer for a long time, and I've never bin able to ketch him a-doin' any good to speak of. He stays overnight and pulls out this mornin'. And he was headed southwards when he left with his posse of bold and ferocious deputies. And while that DHS cowboy that joins up with the Jawbone Smith feller shore needs killin', still, Tex Harmer has bin ripe for a coffin for some time. Dab yore line on that roan hoss, son. He's stout and sound and he'll carry a light-built boy like you a long ways. You kin help ol' 'Gimpy' get his Dutch ovens loaded, then pilot the wagons, and kinda use yore own judgment. Bob Burch will be the wagon pilot and it might do you some good to ride along with Bob. He knows the country up ahead."

Boone looked at the big trail boss. He knew what this bewhiskered man with blue eyes was doing for him. Tex Harmer had described Boone, and the trail boss was giving the boy a chance to make a get-away. He was staking him to a fresh horse, and the wagon pilot would tell him the trail to the north.

"You said you was short-handed," said Boone. "I'd like to go up the trail with you. I'll play my string out. I'll do my best to make a hand."

"Tex Harmer might circle back this way."

"He won't ketch me a-runnin', when he does. I'm almighty obliged for what you said, and I ain't ever forgettin'. But if you can use me, I will stay on with the outfit. And I ain't a-runnin' from Tex Harmer or any man. I'm done a-playin' coyote."

"Then snare out that stockin'-legged black pony and save the roan. Yo're hired. And if Tex Harmer shows up, he won't win too much. You see, a feller fetched me a letter from Uncle Jake Meadows at Red Rock. Jake and me is old pardners. In this letter he says somethin' about a kid with yore kind of face and eyes and manners that might show up. And I was to give you what you needed because you was deservin' of it. So just ketch that black pony and come on along. You kin help Bob Burch and that cross-grained ol' pot rassler to-day. Just make a hand at whatever there is to be done."

So once again Boone held down a job with a trail herd. The big trail boss, whom the boys all called "Jawn R.", was a good beef man and had the knack of getting work out of his cowboys without ever getting cranky. He was good-natured and understanding. And the times when things went bad were the times when Jawn R. grinned the widest.

In the days that followed, when Boone followed the trail herd into Montana, the boy kept watching for Tex Harmer to show

51

up. Tex Harmer or Jawbone. He slept lightly of a night and with his hand close to his gun. And when he rode along in the dust and sun, bringing up the drags, his gaze kept shifting along the sky line, looking for strange riders.

Now and then a couple or more cowboys drifting back south after delivering a herd would stop at the DHS camp. They brought the bits of gossip of the long cattle trail. Mostly their talk was of shooting scrapes and gambling winnings. And of gold. Placer gold that the miners were washing from the creeks. Last Chance Gulch and Virginia City. Now and then a cowhand would have one of those nuggets, and at one of the towns they passed through, Boone saw a gambler with a watch chain made of the raw nuggets. And one of the dance-hall girls wore a necklace of matched nuggets, gift of some placer miner who had struck it rich.

Up in the Black Hills men were becoming fabulously rich. Many a cowboy was swapping his saddle for a pick and shovel and gold pan. It was sometimes hard to get cowboys to work for thirty dollars a month when miners were washing as high as a hundred dollars a day. There were some wild tales of these boom camps.

Tales of sluice boxes being robbed and prospectors murdered. And while it was twenty years before that the Vigilantes had hung Henry Plummer and George Ives and their murderous band, still they had not succeeded in altogether wiping out the lawless element. Stage coaches carrying express boxes were still being waylaid by the road agents. Express messengers were being killed. Passengers were robbed of their gold. And there was still plenty of gold being taken from the hills of Montana and Dakota.

Some of the men who had made a fortune in the gold rush had quietly put that wealth into big stock ranches. They were buying cattle from Texas and Oregon and raising fine horses. The cattle industry was at its peak in the Northwest. Cow towns were lively. Gamblers were reaping a fat harvest. The boothills were filled with graves of men who died with their boots on and their guns smoking.

And Boone, at the beginning of manhood, rode into this wild, reckless life with a quiet sort of smile that might have been an example to many an older man. To Jawn R. he was something of a puzzle.

"Don't you like to raise heck, ever, Boone?"

"Whisky makes me sick. I reckon my stummick wasn't built right. I'd like to dance, only I never did learn how. And I ain't much of a gambler. You see, until I hit the DHS camp, I'd never bin free to do like I wanted. And by the time I was shut of Jawbone, I was too old to learn how. I can't recollect ever havin' laughed out loud."

It was hard for Boone to join in the rough play of the other cow punchers. Oversensitive to any kind of ridicule, he was always afraid of their well-meant but oftentimes brutal gibes. He drank with them and bought the drinks when it came his turn. He tried to learn to dance with the women who mingled with the men in the frontier dance halls. He would sit in a card game or buck the wheel or faro bank. He did his best to be one of them, but it was slow work. He choked on his raw whisky and they joshed him. When he danced, he stumbled clumsily in his heavy cowhide boots, and once he was left standing in the middle of the dance floor by a lady who told him, with vitriolic tongue, that life was too short for even a percentage girl to be stomped to death by clodhoppers.

Crimson with embarrassment, Boone

had quit the dance floor, only to be hauled to the bar by his rough-tongued companions. They teased him without mercy, and he pretended not to mind. But for days afterward he would grow hot with shame at the memory of that humiliation.

One evening, shortly before the trail herd reached Miles City, a couple of cow punchers rode into camp. They were from the SL outfit and were starting for home.

Boone was glad to see them and heard news of Till Driscoll and the other boys. They talked far into the night. And before they quit the fire and sought their blankets, one of them called Boone aside.

"Jawbone is somewhere up in this country, Boone. One of the boys was at Bannock and see him there, drunk and ugly, with two-three other gents that looked like a bad lot. And just a few days ago, at Miles City, I run into Tex Harmer. He was askin' about you. Said he was killin' you on sight. I figgered you'd ought to know. Tex ain't like the other Harmer boys. He's snaky."

"I'll be a-watchin' for him," Boone said quietly.

Chapter 6

Boone Steps Out

The DHS herd was going on to the north side of the Missouri River to a valley east of the Little Rockies. But they would lay over a day at Miles City to get grub and give the cowboys a chance to celebrate and get the dust out of their throats.

Boone rode into town with the other cowboys. He had said nothing to Jawn R. or to any one about Tex Harmer being in that section of the country, because it didn't seem right to Boone that he should be mixing them up in his personal affairs.

They trailed into town by the way of Fort Keogh, and the soldiers helped them put the herd across the Yellowstone. There were also some of the townspeople there to see the herd cross. A sprinkling of women were in the crowd that ate potluck with the DHS boys. Gimpy, nibbling now and then at a smuggled bottle a soldier had fetched from town, was in his glory. He was, for all his physical handicaps that ran the list

56

from a bald head and crossed eyes to a game leg and a walrus moustache, quite a ladies' man. And his son-of-a-gun-in-the-sack was a huge affair of raisins and suet and steamed dough that was his pride. He flavored the sauce with whisky.

And when the dishes rattled in the pan, the DHS cowboys roped out their town horses. Boone caught up his beautiful bay. He had, for obvious reasons, named the bay gelding Get-away, and no horse in the DHS remuda could compare with the sleek bay that had not been saddled since Boone turned him loose the day he hired out to Jawn R.

Boone had shaved and put on his best clothes. He had managed to trade for a pair of hand made boots of soft leather. He had bought some clothes along the trail. And the evening before, he had helped Gimpy around camp, as he often did, and in return the cranky little old cook had trimmed his hair.

So it was that Boone cut a handsome figure as he sat his hot-blooded bay horse. His hat tilted back, his spurs jingling, he was a sight to quicken the pulse beat of any maid. And as they rode past the fort, the ladies grouped on the verandas enthusiastically waved handkerchiefs.

Among the officers' wives and daughters stood the blue-uniformed husbands, and fathers, and brothers. West Pointers, some veterans of the Indian wars, others out of their first frontier post.

There was one among the officers who gave a slight start when Boone rode past on Get-away. He turned to a grizzled officer and said something in a low tone. The older man looked, nodded, and swore softly. And when the cowboys had ridden on to town, these two officers called for their horses.

Boone, his flecked grey eyes always scanning every man's face, leaned idly against the bar. He was watching for Tex Harmer, and his right hand never strayed far from the cedar butt of his gun — the same gun Jawbone had given him.

There was music and laughter. Feet scraped the dance floor to the music of the fiddle. The cowboys, in a festive mood, drank and whooped and in various ways made their most of the brief hours in town.

There were soldiers in the place, and between the soldiers and cowboys there was a none too friendly feeling. The former resented the coming of these cowboys off the trail with money to spend and no military discipline to hold them in check.

Boone paid little attention to the two army officers who came up to the bar. Nor did he give more than a passing glance to the tall civilian who was with them, until this civilian, standing alongside him, pulled back his coat and showed him the sheriff's badge pinned to his shirt.

"I'd be obliged, young man, if you'd step outside with me. I want to have a little powwow. Mebbeso you kin explain it all without any fuss. But don't go pullin' that smoke pole, young man, because yo're well covered."

Boone's eyes hardened. The only DHS man near was old Gimpy, the cook, who was getting as full of whisky as he could. The two army officers crowded closer. Boone smiled crookedly.

"Looks like I'm obliged to do about as you say, sheriff." He walked out with the sheriff, the two officers following close behind. The sheriff led the way across the street to a small cabin above the door on which was a sign, Sheriff's Office.

Inside, Boone faced them, wondering what it was all about. He had not long to wait. The younger of the two army officers faced him with stern military eye.

"You rode into town on a horse that was

stolen from me at Fort Whipple, Arizona. Where did you get the horse? Speak up, and speak the truth!"

"I ain't in the habit of lyin'," said Boone, angered by the army man's tone. "And I'm not a horse thief. And you ain't talkin' to one of yore boot-lickin' soldiers. And if you lay a hand on me, you brass-buttoned dummy, I'll make you danged sorry. I'm free, white, and my own boss. Stand back from me!"

"Better let me handle this, lieutenant," said the sheriff. "Cool off, cowboy."

"My word is as good as his," said Boone. "And I'll lay a bet that Mister Brass Buttons can't even ride the horse. Let him prove that horse is his before he calls me a horse thief. Or, if he's any kind of a sport, I'll make him a bargain. If he can fork that bay horse and ride him down to the end of the street, without grabbin' the saddle-horn, the horse is his."

The sheriff, for various reasons, had little love to waste on army men. The soldiers had caused him plenty of trouble since he had come into office. And when he turned soldier prisoners over to the military authorities, results had been none too satisfactory. He turned to the lieutenant with a wide grin.

"That sounds like a sportin' enough proposition, lieutenant. Are you callin' the bet?"

The officer, a tall, handsome man in his thirties, smile stiffly and nodded.

"I'll call it. Though the captain here can identify the animal. He lost his mount at the same time mine was stolen. However, I'll take up the challenge. Bring the horse over."

"Supposin' you go get him?" said Boone. "I'm no dog robbed servant to any man. Yonder the horse stands. Swing on to him and ride him down the street without pulling leather."

Red with anger, the lieutenant stalked stiffly across the street to the hitch-rack where a score of saddled horses stood. He untied the hackamore rope, and the bay horse whistled softly. A little group of soldiers and cowboys stood around as the officer led the bay horse into the middle of the street.

The lieutenant put a foot in the stirrup. The bay horse whirled and kicked, barely missing the astonished and now furious army man. The officer approached more warily now. A cowboy's call brought a crowd out on to the sidewalk.

The lieutenant had not expected such an

audience. Red-faced, shaking with suppressed anger, he made another more cautious attempt to mount. He was in the saddle. But before he could get the right stirrup, the bay horse dropped his head and jumped sidewise, pitching. The second jump landed the army officer in the dust. Bruised, shaken, he staggered to his feet. The bay horse, whistling, shied back into the other horses and stood there, bridle reins dragging. As the irate officer approached, there was a scramble among the horses. Fearing he would be kicked, the lieutenant halted.

"Go git 'im, buttons," called a cowboy. "He's gentle. Or he'd orter be. I bet his mother was gentle."

The lieutenant managed to grab the trailing hackamore rope. He dragged the horse out into the street and was about to kick the bay in the belly when Boone's voice, rasping, dangerous, halted him.

"Abuse that horse, Mister Lieutenant, and I'll kick the face plumb off you. If he's yourn, get on him and ride him."

Again the lieutenant mounted. The bay horse let him get well seated. Then, with a jerk, he was in the air, bawling, twisting, bucking down the dusty street. The spectators cheered wildly. The officer lost his hat, then a stirrup. He was hanging on with both hands. Now the big bay halted, whirled back, pitched once, and the lieutenant landed on his neck and shoulders in the dirt. He lay there, a twisted, motionless heap. Boone stepped out and caught the trotting bay.

The captain was already sending orders right and left to his men. A mule-drawn ambulance was brought, and the unconscious lieutenant placed in it. The captain, white with rage, turned to the sheriff.

"I demand that this man be placed under arrest."

"On what charges?" asked the sheriff grimly.

"Horse stealing. That's a stolen horse."

The sheriff grinned and shook his head. "I heard the agreement the lad made with the lieutenant. So far as I'm concerned, the boy keeps his horse."

"Then," said the angry army officer, "I'll take the responsibility of having my men make the arrest. He's stolen government property and he's subject to government punishment."

"Hold on," snapped the sheriff. "That cowboy has friends. There they stand a-watchin'. Heaven help the soldiers that try to take that cowhand to yore guard house.

Use some sense. Do you want a free-for-all fight here?"

The captain muttered something and gave some orders to a sergeant. He had lowered his voice so that only the latter heard. The sergeant saluted. The captain got on his horse and rode away in the wake of the ambulance. The sergeant, a beefy, thick-necked, pugnacious-looking man, grinned and swaggered into the saloon. The sheriff crossed over to where Boone and a dozen grinning cowboys stood.

"I don't want trouble, boys," he told them, "but it looks to me like trouble is comin'. That sergeant is the bully of the fort and he'll be up to somethin'. But if trouble comes, keep yore guns in their scabbards. No shootin'. Bust all the noses you want, but keep them shootin' irons outa yore hands. And, young feller, tie that horse and come along with me. Ther's another little matter that needs straightenin' up between me and you."

Boone nodded. He reckoned that, if Tex Harmer had been here, and if Tex Harmer was still town marshal of Red Rock, then he would have given the sheriff a good description of Jawbone and himself. And the sheriff of Miles City now planned to hold him on that bank robbery and murder charge. With sinking heart, he followed the sheriff into the little office.

"Sit down, young man. And keep yore hand off that gun. I want to ask you a few questions."

"Yes, sir?"

"What's yore name?"

"Boone."

"First name?"

"Boone."

"Then what's yore last name?"

"Boone is the only name I got, sheriff."

"Ever bin in Red Rock, Wyoming?"

"Yes, sir."

"Know a man named Jawbone Smith?"

"I do."

"You was his pardner, wasn't you, Boone?"

"Well, sort of. He raised me."

"Where was you the afternoon that the Red Rock bank was held up and two men killed?"

"I was at camp. So was Jawbone. That is the truth, sir."

"Got any way of provin' what you say, son?"

"No, sir, I haven't."

"Then," said the sheriff, rising and walking to the open door, "if I was a-wearin' yore boots, I'd get out of this part of the country. The climate here don't suit yore clothes." And without another word, the sheriff left Boone alone.

For a few minutes Boone sat there. He knew that the only sensible thing to do was to follow the kindly sheriff's advice. Tex Harmer was somewhere in the vicinity, ready to make trouble. Besides, there was that ruckus over the bay horse that was not yet settled, by any means. Boone knew that Jawbone must have stolen the two bay horses or had bargained for them with money or gun, and at any rate, coming down to cases, he was riding a stolen horse. Miles City was not a healthy climate just now. Boone decided to hunt up Jawn R., draw what little pay he had coming, and drag it.

With that intention in mind, he crossed the street and walked into the saloon. He saw Jawn R. standing at the far end of the bar. As he started toward where the trail boss stood, some one bumped into him. It was the beefy sergeant. Boone started to walk past the man, who staggered tipsily. But the sergeant again bumped him, leering into his face. Some soldiers standing around laughed jeeringly at Boone's attempt to pass the burly sergeant, who now deliberately spat at Boone's boots.

Boone's face went white. With a leap, he was on the sergeant. The two went down with a crash. The soldiers formed a thick circle.

Old Gimpy had seen the thing start. So, also, had the sheriff. Gimpy's creaky voice went up in a shout:

"They got the Boone kid! Come on, cowboys!"

Now the tall sheriff was shoving through the ring of soldiers. They refused to give way and the law officer's gun barrel cracked against three or four heads in a workmanlike manner.

Boone fought with the fury of a panther pitted against a grizzly. Ripping, tearing, punishing with teeth and hands and knees, he was giving the burly, bull-dogging sergeant a tough battle. Boone, for all his slender build, was made of whalebone and hard rubber. His hands gripped the soldier's throat, steel springs clamping on the thick neck. As the sergeant fought to shake free, Boone wriggled from underneath and now fought from on top. He pounded the man's head on the floor. Now, letting go with one hand, regardless of the jolting fists that pounded his ribs, he drove his left fist again and again into the beefy face. The crunch of the blows was sickening. A soldier stepped close, his foot swinging to kick Boone. Jawn R. grabbed the man, picked him up, pitched him across the heads of the crowd. His falling body struck a table and he lay there, whining like a whipped dog, under the wreckage.

The swift ferocity of Boone's attack had given him the advantage. Not for the fraction of an instant did he quit fighting, fists and teeth, his hands gripping and shaking that battered head. Now he gripped the sergeant's thick black hair and pounded the bruised face into the sawdust. Snarling like a dog, his face livid and distorted, he beat the man into insensibility. He was still snarling and sobbing when Jawn R. and the sheriff pulled him off. There were half a dozen other fights in progress now. Jawn R. and the sheriff held the struggling Boone. At the sheriff's orders, the saloon man threw a bucket of water in Boone's face. The shock of the water brought the boy back to his senses. Now, between Jawn R. and the lanky sheriff, he began pulling soldiers and cowboys apart. A few minutes of swift labour put the place in order. The sheriff was shoving soldiers out of the place. Then he dragged the battered, half-conscious sergeant to the bar. A nod to the bartender and a pail of water was sloshed in the bruised, swollen face. The sheriff gripped the sergeant's shoulder.

"The next time you start a free-for-all in this town, I'll slam you in jail and keep you there till you rot. And yore tin-soldier friends won't git you out, either. I've took about all I can stand from you drunken bums. Now get outa town and stay out. I'm postin' every saloon in town to put you on the Injun list. Tell that to the damn-fool officer that ribbed this deal. Get!"

He spun the sergeant around and kicked him out. Then he turned to Boone.

"Time you was gettin' along yore trail, son."

Now a tall, white-haired, white-moustached army officer came striding into the place. His face was set and stern-looking.

"Did my men start this, sheriff?"

"I reckon they did, colonel."

"Give me their names and I'll see that they don't do it again!"

"I don't reckon the ringleader will have much taste for fightin' again for some time."

"H-m-m-m-m. I saw Sergeant Mulligan come out the door somewhat abruptly. He's a good stable sergeant, but he can't stay clear of trouble. He's licked every man at the post one time or another. Who trimmed his wick, sheriff?"

The sheriff grinned and pointed to Boone. The colonel looked astounded. "Not really?"

"Saloon rules. He was all over Mulligan. I never saw the beat of it."

"I'll be back in a few minutes, sheriff."

The colonel strode to the door. He called the soldiers outside to attention. And then, in words that blistered and cut and ripped, the veteran officer laid down the law. When he was done, he dismissed them and sent them back to their barracks. Then he came back to the saloon, and, stepping to the bar, ordered drinks for the house.

"Where's the lad that fought Mulligan?" he asked the sheriff.

The sheriff looked around. "He seems to be gone, colonel."

"Too bad! I wanted to shake hands with him. Well, sheriff, I'm sorry my men have caused you trouble again. I've blessed 'em out from Arizona to Montana, but they'll keep on getting into fights just the same. Well, here's to better results!"

"How's the lieutenant?"

"Broken collar bone, the young idiot! What happened? He wouldn't say much except that he had a drink too many and tried to ride a horse that belonged to a DHS cowboy. And Captain Draper was just as reticent. Odd. Damned odd." And so this veteran of the Indian campaigns dismissed an unpleasant subject.

Meanwhile Boone and Jawn R. rode to the DHS camp. The boy held out his hand to the trail boss.

"Time I was movin' along, Jawn R. Looks like I bring nothin' but bad luck wherever I go."

"I heard about Tex Harmer bein' at Miles City. And I ain't askin' which way yo're a-headin'. But all us boys wish you good luck. And if you want a winter job, I'll have one for you. Good luck, Boone."

Chapter 7

Beaver Brown

Once more adrift along a lonely trail, Boone headed northward. He was getting rid of that feeling of lonesomeness. It was good to be riding along on a good horse, not knowing what he would find beyond the sky line. In his saddle pockets were a sack of salt, a few clean clothes, a butcher knife, shells for his six-shooter, and the 45-70 Winchester he had traded his bed for. He was young and strong and filled with the spirit of high adventure.

He sang as he rode along. Yonder circled a bunch of antelope. There were buffalo over to the eastward. The country abounded in wild game. The grass in the coulees touched his stirrups. The creeks were filled with water. This was cow country as yet unmarred by a strand of barbed wire. Boone camped that night with a trapper. The trapper was on his way north to the Canadian fur country. A garrulous, long-haired, bearded man, given to talking to himself. He seemed a little brain-cracked. But he was interesting to listen to. He had been all over the Western country, and had lived with Jim Bridger and Bill Williams and "Liver Eatin'" Johnson. He'd been a government scout. He asked the boy's name.

"Boone?" he repeated when he heard the name. "Boone, eh? I knowed Dan'l Boone. You ain't kin to him?"

"I don't know. I was raised by a man named Jawbone Smith."

"Eh? How's that again? Jawbone Smith, you say? Tell me, what kind of a lookin' feller is yore Jawbone Smith?"

When Boone had described him, the trapper sat there, nodding and muttering, his eyes like fox's eyes under saggy ragged brows.

"Ye wouldn't know, boy, where a man'd be likely to run on to Jawbone? I ain't seen him in years. I knowed him years ago. Knowed him better than most men ever knowed him. I'd be proud to locate him. Aye, sonny, that I would. And wouldn't he be su'prised to see his old pardner, 'Beaver' Brown! Did he ever speak of Beaver Brown to you?"

"Not as I recollect."

The trapper chuckled. "Likely he

73

wouldn't. Close with his words, ol' Jawbone. And for danged good reasons. He'll hang in the end, and there'll be fire a-waitin' for him. I'd shore love to cut his sign! Ye know aught of his whereabouts, boy?"

"I reckon he's in Montana somewheres."

The trapper, dressed in greasy buckskin, peered hard at the boy, until Boone felt uncomfortable under the stare of those twinkling eyes.

"Boone, ye say? Boone, eh? And ye know no other name? It's odd. Danged if it ain't odd! Boone? And he raised you from a pup, eh? Hauled you around with him wherever he went. Beat ye, no doubt, and treated ye ornery, and ye run off when ye got enough to make the get-away. And he called ye Boone —"

The trapper chuckled and muttered as he sat gazing into the camp fire. Boone wanted to ask him some questions, but something told him that he would get no answer.

"I'd like almighty much," Boone ventured, "to know who I really am. Who my folks were, and everything."

"So ye would," chuckled Beaver, "and like as not ye'll die a-wonderin'. And there's this, laddie, to consider. For all ye know, ye might be a heap sight better off for not knowin' about yer folks. Think that un over keerful, for there's meat in it. Aye, meat! And mayhap it's meat that's tainted. Ye're a likely lookin' colt. What need have you to know aught of who or what yer father before ye was. Boone's a name to be proud of. Live up to the name Dan'l Boone bore and ye'll never stray far wrong. Though it's contrary learnin' ye got from my old pardner, Jawbone. Ye wouldn't be knowin', what part of Montana ol' Jawbone 'u'd be at? Ye wouldn't hold back the knowledge on ol' Beaver? Him as et and slept and emptied many a jug at the same fire with Jawbone Smith? Ye wouldn't lie, laddie?"

"I don't know where he is," said Boone, uneasy under the glitter of the foxlike eyes, "any more than you do. He may be dead, for all I know."

"To share just one more camp with ol' Jawbone," the trapper chuckled in grisly fashion, his unwashed, bony fingers whetting a curved-bladed skinning knife, "with a jug full of likker, and meat in the pan. Takin' drink for drink with him. The coyotes a-singin' the same as ye hear 'em sing to-night." He ran his thumb down the whetted blade and chuckled unpleasantly. Boone shuddered at the expression on the bearded face.

After a time he left the trapper sitting

there by the dying fire, took his saddle blanket, and bedded down some distance away. He slept lightly, his hand on his gun.

Some time during the night Boone awoke with a start. Against the pale sky, not ten feet from where he lay, crouched the trapper, a long-barrelled rifle in his hands. But the trapper was not looking at him. He was staring into the night. Boone heard hoofbeats and the sound of voices. Then, not two hundred yards away, he saw four men riding single file, their horses at a long trot. Boone, his gun ready, watched. There was something in the manner in which the leader sat his saddle that reminded Boone of Tex Harmer. It was with a sigh of great relief that the boy saw them ride on without discovering the camp. Now the trapper called to him in a cautious tone.

"Awake, laddie?"

"Yes."

"Ye seen 'em ride past, eh? Huntin' for somebody, mayhap. Seems to me ye might be knowin' who they're a-huntin', eh?"

Boone made no reply. The trapper chuckled softly. Boone pulled on his boots. Sleep now was out of the question. He reckoned it must be about two hours till daylight. And he wanted to be as far away as possible by the time the sun came up.

He made up his mind that until he had shaken off Tex Harmer, he would travel at night and hide in the daytime. The trapper made no comment when Boone saddled his bay horse.

"The sheepdog," said Beaver, "never travels with the wolf. There was one wolf, anyhow, among them four. My trigger finger shore itched when he rid past, skylighted sweet and purty. Then, thinks I, if ye knock him over, Beaver, ye'll be interferin' with fate. And if the other three is likewise wolves, they'll be doin' some shootin', and I ain't quite ready for to meet my Maker. So I lets the wolf go, much as I'd hanker for to see his pelt hung on the fence. And then I see ye settin' there awake. And I wonders a leetle concernin' the connection of them four wolves and the laddie as goes by the name of Boone and was raised up by my ol' pardner Jawbone. A close shave, laddie. Aye, close! Ye be a-doin' right to be travellin'! There's too much open country betwixt here and the badlands. Put it behind ye as quick as yer hoss can pack ye there. Hit the river at Crooked Crik."

"Thanks, Beaver, I'll head that a way. You say you know one of them four? Which one?"

"The one as rode in the lead. Him as killed a pardner of mine once, down in Texas. His name is Tex Harmer and he's as poison' as a rattler. Ye've heard of him and his cousins, mebby? The Harmers as own the Y Down iron on the Pecos. Tex, cousin to the other boys, is the he-wolf of the pack. They tell me he taken a job as town marshal of Red Rock so he'd be able to kill off some folks he hated. Which he's done. But seems like it was said Jawbone was on his list. I'll ask ye no questions and ye'll tell ol' Beaver no lies. But when ye come up with Jawbone, tell him ye saw me and I was as spry as a two-year-old. And that I'll be a-cuttin' his sign one of these days. Ride keerful — Boone. Boone's the name. The same as Dan'l Boone's. Yep, Boone'd be the name. So long." Chuckling, Beaver crawled into his dingy blankets.

Boone, the trapper's words drumming in his ears, rode away. And he rode on through the night with the feeling that Beaver, had he so chosen, might have unravelled some of the mystery surrounding his parentage. He had even hinted that the secret was an ugly one, much better left in its grave. Puzzled, upset in his mind, Boone rode at a long trot.

Chapter 8

Hold-up!

It was drizzling rain at daybreak. Dawn, gray and dismal, found Boone dropping off a ridge and into a long coulee that led to a creek heavily fringed with tall willows and cottonwoods. He was soaking wet and shivering with cold. A raw wind bit through to the bone. He wore no slicker and his coat was a soggy thing. He wished that he dared risk a fire. The rain-drenched blackness, just before dawn, and the leaning of his horse away from the wind, had confused the boy's sense of direction. He was lost. And he did not know whether or not he had passed Tex Harmer and his three men.

Now, across the creek, coming down a muddy, yellow road, came a six-horse stage on its way to Miles City. Boone rode into some willows to wait until it passed. He could hear the rattle of the harness, the creak of the brakes as the driver swung his team down the slope to the creek crossing. The stage looked a little weird, there

79

in the wet, gray dawn, its horses wet, mud-spattered, swinging at a trot. The driver and express messenger on the box. The curtains of the coach tightly buttoned. The coach swaying and pitching on its leather springs, rolling like a barrel on waves.

Now, just as the six-horse stage dropped out of sight in the trees and brush, there came the sound of a shot. Then more shots in rapid succession. A screech of brake blocks. Above the other noises, the terri-fied scream of a woman.

Boone jumped his bay horse down the slope. He saw four men on horseback, shrouded in black slickers, their faces cov-ered with black handkerchiefs, guns levelled. One of the men swayed in his saddle. From inside the coach came the woman's fright-ened screams. The driver sat with his hands raised, lines wrapped around the brake. Beside him slumped the express messenger, shot through the head.

"Kick off the box!" called one of the road agents. "Be quick! Bill, shut that dang woman's yelling! Drag her and the others out and we'll see what they got to fill the hat."

Boone wondered afterward what prompted him to do what he now did. Jumping his horse into the brush, he leaped off and scrambled up among some boulders. He rested his rifle across a rock. Now one of the road agents dismounted and strode toward the buttoned curtains. His arm lifted to jerk the curtain open. Boone's rifle cracked, and the man fell back with a startled howl. Boone shot again, and the man who seemed to be the leader whirled his horse, cursing. The man who had been swaying drunkenly, now slid to the ground and lay in the mud, doubled up.

The man on foot climbed back on his horse. Boone's gun was sending heavy slugs around their heads. Now a gun barked from inside the coach. The three men, leaving their badly wounded companion, raced for shelter. Boone's bullets drove them northward, along the road down which the coach had come. Boone yelled to the driver.

"Whip up, man! Whip up!"

But a man tore aside the curtain and jumped out. He picked the wounded man out of the mud and shoved him inside the coach. Then he nodded to the driver.

"Get going!"

As the stage coach climbed the slope, Boone stood up and waved. They were passing within fifty feet of him. The passenger, a well-dressed, middle-aged man, called to the driver to stop.

"I want to talk to you, sir!" called the passenger. But Boone waved them on.

"I'll ketch up to you!" he called, and started for his horse. The driver, eager to quit the place, cracked his long buckskin lash.

Boone got his horse and followed the stage coach. He caught it at the top of the slope.

Chapter 9

Virginia Lee

The driver had pulled up to wind his team. The passenger got out, and through the partly opened curtains Boone caught a glimpse of a white-faced young lady. The man, with a grim smile, held his hand out.

"That was a very brave thing to do, sir. You've saved a government pay roll, and you've saved my life and the honour of my daughter. I am Judge Lee of Fort Benton. Making a business trip. I was asleep when they attacked the coach. And when your bullet struck that brute in the shoulder, you saved me from killing him. Let's see what can be done for the guard. Then we'll take a look at this man inside. He's dying."

"The guard is dead," said the driver. "But he shore lived long enough to get one of 'em before he was plugged."

Boone stepped to the side of the coach.

"This is my daughter, Virginia. Daughter, this is the gentleman who came to our rescue."

"The name is Boone," said the boy.

"Boone?" For a moment a strange light flickered in the deep-set eyes of the judge. "Virginia, this is Mr. Boone."

Boone flushed under the direct gaze of this girl. She was holding out her hand and trying to smile in spite of her recent fright and horror of that mud-soiled, red-smeared man who lay at her feet.

It was the first time in his life that the boy had ever met a well-brought-up woman. And this girl with hazel eyes and soft, brown hair that curled about her cameo face was the loveliest thing Boone had ever seen, even in his dreams. He took her hand awkwardly. Then, to cover his confusion, he turned his attention to the wounded man.

The man, dying perhaps, but unwhimpering, looked into Boone's face. A crooked smile of recognition twisted his tight-lipped mouth.

"The SL kid, or I'm blind! Howdy, kid. I seen you at Abilene the night Jawbone killed Bob Harmer. I was with the Y Down trail herd. Now I'm cashin' in my last chips. I tried for big coin and got a bullet. And that Texas son of a snake rode off without even sayin' 'so long.' He didn't know if I was bad hit. Nor he didn't care.

Gosh, I'd like a slug of whisky."

Judge Lee handed Boone an uncorked flask. The dying man drank. His eyes were getting glassy.

"Obliged, gents. Kid, watch Tex. He's after you. He'll kill you, the snake! Dang him for ridin' off without makin' a try to save a man!"

"Tex Harmer was one of yore bunch?" asked Boone.

"He was the big boss. . . . Another drink. . . . So long, button. . . . Just a cowboy . . . done wrong. . . ."

He was dead. They covered him up with a horse blanket. The judge shook his head sadly. "Just a cowboy!"

After a moment, Judge Lee turned to Boone. "There's a fortune in that box up in the boot. The guard is dead. The driver is unharmed. I have only a derringer pistol. I would make it well worth your while if you could go on with us to Miles City. Those men may follow. Or there may be others waiting somewhere along the road. Name your price, sir."

"We might talk about that later, sir," said Boone. "I'll ride alongside as far as Miles City."

"My daughter and I will never forget your courtesy, Mr. Boone." He smiled.

"You are a brave gentleman."

Boone shook his head. "Just a cowboy, sir. Like him that lays under that blanket."

He mounted his bay horse. Judge Lee handed him a heavy coat. He also made him take a big drink of whisky. The rain still swept the country in a dismal downpour.

In spite of the rain, Judge Lee and his daughter preferred to ride on the seat with the driver. The two dead men were inside.

Now, a horseman, leading two pack mules, loomed up out of the drizzle, and Boone relaxed his grip on his gun when he recognized Beaver. The trapper looked sharply at the boy, then up at the judge and his daughter riding in the rain. As the stage rolled along, Boone paused to chat a minute with Beaver. In a few words he told of the hold-up. And how Judge Lee had asked him to ride as escort back to Miles City.

The trapper, chuckling and muttering into his beard, nodded his shaggy head and rubbed a long nose between thumb and forefinger.

"Fate! The workin' of fate, mind what I'm tellin' ye. Lee's a power. More'n likely he'll be governor of the State. Ye done him a big favour. Fer Tex Harmer's a killer, and

Heaven help the woman whose face or figger strikes his ugly fancy! If Judge Lee has got gratitude in him, he'll be the makin' of ye, laddie. . . . God's fate, a-workin' out things. If he offers ye a chance to make somethin' of yerself, take it. Take it, laddie, for it's God's fate." Beaver rode on into the rain, mumbling and chuckling.

Boone caught up with the stage. The girl smiled down at him. She was wrapped up until only her face, red-cheeked now, misted with rain, showed. The judge leaned down.

"Who was that old character?"

"A trapper named Beaver Brown. I stopped at his camp last night."

"Beaver Brown. I believe that if he shaved that beard off and trimmed his hair, and perhaps bathed in soap and hot water, I'd known him by another name than Beaver Brown. His eyes are peculiar. I've certainly seen him somewhere."

From the way he said it, Boone drew the conclusion that the meeting that was vague in the judge's memory had been an unpleasant one. Judge Lee was scowling thoughtfully. Boone rode on ahead, his quick eyes scanning the brush or boulders that might conceal a second party of highwaymen. And in his mind was the knowledge that Tex Harmer was a road agent.

They had a hot dinner that noon at a stage station. There, the dead men were left, and the judge and his daughter rode inside once more. Boone tied his horse alongside one of the wheelers and rode up on the driver's box, his rifle across his lap. The fresh horses stepped out at a lively gait. There was a new driver handling the reins. From him Boone learned that Judge Lee was a man of wealth. Banker and cattle owner at Fort Benton. He was a circuit judge who travelled about, hearing cases of importance appealed from lower court. And he was now on his way to hold court at Miles City. He had been a member of the Vigilantes and had stood for stern justice. A Virginian by birth, Judge Lee had lived in Texas, had been dragged into a feud down there, and had left the Lone Star State after killing a man in a duel. The man killed was a political enemy and former schoolmate in Virginia. The duel that had cost one man his life and from which Lee barely escaped death, had all but wrecked him. It was said that he never quite recovered from the wound that barely missed his heart. And that he had never forgiven himself for taking the life of a man who had once been a friend of his childhood, though that man was somewhat of a blackguard and a notorious gambler and duellist. A fiery-tempered quick-triggered scion of cavalier stock.

The stage driver was an old Texan who had come north with the first trail herds. He was a talkative sort, and like many of his calling as stage driver, was an oral news vendor. Boone listened, content to let the other do the talking.

Dusk brought them into Miles City. They pulled up at the stage station with a flourish. The face of the tall sheriff, as Boone handed down the strong box, was a study. Boone climbed down and was about to unbutton the curtains of the coach when he was brushed aside. A tall army officer with one arm in a sling was performing that task, and with easy grace and formal manner was helping Virginia Lee to the board walk. He shook hands warmly with her and the judge. Boone backed away, red in the face, and helped the sheriff lug the strong box into the office where some soldiers waited. Boone had recognized the tall officer as the lieutenant who had claimed his bay horse.

Now the colonel came up in a mule-drawn rig and he took the judge's daughter in his arms and kissed her warmly. She called him Uncle Jim. He handed her up into the rig, then greeted the judge with bluff heartiness. But before the judge allowed the colonel to place him in the rig, he came into the office.

Inside, the lieutenant stood stiffly, his eyes staring at Boone, who was shedding his raincoat.

"Ah, Boone, I was afraid you'd gone. Could I ask you to stay over in town tonight? I'll be in, first thing in the morning. There is something I wish to talk over with you. It will be well worth your while to stay over. I'll try to thank you, then, for the great service you have done my daughter, and me, and your government." He slapped the lieutenant on the back.

"Harry, I want you to shake hands with a friend of mine. Mr. Boone, Lieutenant Clanton. You two should know one another."

"Mr. Boone," said the lieutenant, smiling thinly, "and I have met." He turned to his men and gave them the order to take the strong box. And he marched stiffly out behind them. Judge Lee's brows lifted, but he said nothing. He shook hands with Boone, then left with a nod to the sheriff.

"Now," said the lanky sheriff, "let's go over and have a drink, young feller. And you tell me what all this is about. I'm danged if I can make head or tail of it."

Boone grinned crookedly. He was chilled, and hungry, and tired. Something that had been singing in his heart had quit singing. He called himself a fool for even hoping that a girl like that would trouble to say goodbye to a roving cowboy who didn't even have manners.

"A drink," he said gruffly, "will do some good. Another one will do more good. I reckon, sheriff, I'll get tight as a fiddler. Then I'll drift along."

The sheriff started to say something, then changed his mind. He smiled to himself and said nothing. He had not missed that little bit of drama outside, when Lieutenant Clanton had brushed Boone aside.

Chapter 10

A Friendly Sheriff

Over his third drink, Boone made a wry face and set down the glass.

"I reckon, sheriff," he said shamefacedly, "that I never was cut out to be a drinkin' man. I'd a heap ruther eat some supper."

The tall sheriff nodded. "Supper she is, and I'm buyin' it. And if every man figgered as grub was better than whisky for his system, this job of mine 'u'd simmer down to nothin'. I'd keep me a box or two of indigestion pills on hand and buy me a lunch stand on the side."

At supper Boone gave him the story of the stage hold-up. The sheriff listened in silence.

"I didn't like that Harmer gent's looks nor his ways," said the law officer, "and I didn't put much stock in what he said about you bein' mixed in that bank robbery. And when I sized you up, I knowed that there was somethin' wrong with Harmer's story. You ain't a thief. Not with that pair of eyes in your head. Even if you are forkin' a stolen hoss." He grinned widely.

"He thinks I am."

"Who thinks you are?"

"That smart-aleck lieutenant. And he'll tell Judge Lee and the lady."

"Don't be so sure about that. Lieutenant Clanton ain't a bad young feller. And he ain't a long-tongued tale tattler. And even if he was to come right out and accuse you, that's no sign Judge Lee is gonna believe it. Lee's business is to judge the guilty from the innocent and he's mighty good at it. And there's no denyin' you done him and his gal a mighty big turn. I bet he'll do somethin' for you, boy."

Boone's eyes clouded. "I can make my own way. I'm askin' no favors of any man."

For all his appearance of being a grown man, Boone was pretty much of a boy in many ways. His moodiness now was the sulkiness of a boy whose sensitive nature has been hurt. Perhaps the sheriff understood, for he said nothing. He must have known that anything he could say would aggravate rather than relieve the boy's injured feelings.

"You aim to pull out in the mornin', son?"

"I reckon."

Boone, before he had done anything else, had stabled and cared for his horse. The bay would be rested enough by morning to carry him a distance from town. Away from the girl who had not thought to say goodbye.

"There's nothin' much around here to hold a young feller with ambitions," admitted the sheriff. "Just cow outfits. A thirty-a-month job ain't much in the way of pilin' up a fortune or gettin' ahead. Got much schoolin'?"

"None. Only what I've taught myself, and what Uncle Jake, the postmaster at Red Rock, showed me. He says I learn quick enough but that I'd ought to go to school."

"I got a brother who has an outfit over on the Teton. He's got a slew of young uns, his oldest about your age. They keep a schoolmaster there at the ranch, wintertimes. He could use you if I sent him a letter. And while you was helpin' around the ranch, you'd get time to study."

"I'd work for my board," said Boone earnestly, "if I could get some book learnin' that a way."

"You'll get wages. And you'll earn 'em. But wintertimes, the days are short and the evenin's long. After you'd done shovelin' hay and ridin' out after pore cows, you'd get plenty time to read and study. You got it in you to learn fast. Besides, there's plenty of young folks around there and they have good times. Dances and such. I don't reckon you was ever around young folks much?"

"No, sir. None, you might say."

"Well, you'll shore have a good time, then. Once you get to know them, you'll have a good time. Saloons and gamblin' houses is no place for a boy. Especially a boy as don't care for that life. I'll fix you up a letter."

They went over to the sheriff's office and the kindly officer wrote a lengthy letter to his brother who had a ranch on the Teton. Boone did not know where the Teton was.

"It's near Fort Benton. The home ranch is only about thirty miles from town. When you get to Benton, ask anybody where Ken Hanley's place is."

"Judge Lee lives at Fort Benton," said Boone.

"So he does," replied the sheriff, trying to appear unconcerned. "And so does lots of other fine folks. The kind of folks you'll want to throw in with. Folks that is makin' Montana history. They're plain folks, son. No frills. Most of 'em was in here when the Injuns was on the warpath. They've been hungry and cold and scared and broke. It takes things like that to put big hearts in folks. It gives 'em understanding and tolerance and takes the mean poison outa their systems. You've been seein' too much orneriness, son. It's time you got among your own kind of people."

And for a long time Bill Hanley, sheriff of Miles City, talked to the range waif who sat listening. And when daylight came, he was at the stable to shake hands with Boone and wish him good luck.

Boone had been gone about an hour when Judge Lee and his daughter drove up in an army hack.

"The boy's pulled out, judge," said the sheriff, in reply to the judge's inquiry.

Judge Lee looked disappointed. His daughter bit her lip. Virginia Lee had come to town with her father to see the young cowboy and to be there when her father told Boone that he had a good opening for him on the Lee Ranch.

"That boy is mighty proud, judge. Reminds me of a thoroughbred colt that's been badly handled. And it's goin' to take a lot of doggoned careful handlin' to keep him from bein' outlaw. He's high-strung and quick to feel a hurt. And he is high-headed in matters that touch his pride."

96

"Who is he, sheriff? Where did he come from?"

"He's called Boone. Near as I can learn, he was raised by an outlaw called Jawbone Smith. Kicked around and led into bad company. He come up from Texas with the trail herds."

"Boone is not a common name," said Judge Lee. "I knew some Boones in the South. I'd like to talk to the boy. He must know something about his childhood."

The sheriff shook his head. "Jawbone raised him from the time he can remember, so he told me. But Jawbone ain't any kin to him."

"I'd like to find him."

"You'll find him, mebbe, when you get back to Fort Benton, judge. I sent him over to my brother Ken's place, Ken Hanley."

"Ken's place is next to mine. I didn't know you were Ken's brother. He's one of my best friends, sheriff. My dearest neighbor."

The sheriff's eyes crinkled at the corners. "I knowed that, judge, when I sent him. Ken's a great hand with young colts. And his wife is the motherin' kind. She'll give the boy that motherin' he's missed."

"Martha Hanley," said Judge Lee, removing his big black hat, "is one of the finest women God ever put on earth to comfort men. My first winter in Montana, sheriff, was a black one. My wife died and I was left with the baby. There were nights when I quit believing in God. And God knows what might have become of me if it had not been for Martha Hanley. She's the only mother my little girl ever knew. And she and Ken saved me from a fate that, when I look back upon it, makes me shudder. And you are Ken Hanley's brother. Sir, I am indeed proud to shake your hand. And I am mighty glad you sent the Boone boy to them."

Judge Lee had stepped out of the rig and had gone inside the sheriff's office. It was in there, alone, that they had talked. Now the judge came to the door to tell Virginia that she need not wait for him. Court opened at ten, and he had business to attend to before going to the court-house.

But Lieutenant Clanton had ridden up and he smile and saluted the judge.

"If you'll trust me with the honor, sir, I'll keep Virginia busy while you're in town. Provided, of course, that she'll allow me that privilege."

"I don't reckon she'll mind," smiled the judge.

"Don't be too positive, sir. She ran off

this morning." But he must have been fairly confident of his company being acceptable, for he turned his horse over to an orderly and climbed into the hack, taking the lines from the driver.

"Harry," said the girl, "you shouldn't be driving with only one good arm. These mules bolted twice when we were coming in."

"Lady," said the young lieutenant, "I drove the fastest trotting team in Nashville. I think I can handle a span of army mules."

As the driver stepped down, the young officer drove down the street at a lively clip and out along the open road.

The corporal who had been supplanted as driver of the mules looked after them, smiling faintly. Then he went into the nearest saloon.

"If I wasn't broke," he told the bartender, "I'd bet a month's pay that there's a team of mules that's gonna scatter a shavetail and his best gal and a new gover'ment rig all over the flats before noon. That looie might 'a' drove the fastest trotter in Nashville, but he never rode behind them two mouse-coloured, long-eared hunks of muleflesh when they took it into their heads to run. If he had six good arms, they wouldn't be half enough to handle them ribbons. Gimme a beer."

Chapter 11

Roped!

As the trail to Fort Benton was a long one and he had ridden the stout-hearted bay across a good many miles since he left the DHS camp, two days before, Boone rode at a leisurely gait. He planned to take it easy. So it was that he had not gone very many miles along the road when he heard the clatter of wagon wheels and saw a fast-moving cloud of dust behind him. He saw the canvas-covered rig, drawn by a pair of runaway mules, careen and bump over the rough ground as the team quit the road. They had come up out of a draw and were now tearing across the prairie.

Boone growled impatiently as he swung the big bay around. He had little love for things military, and his experience at Miles City had left a bad taste in his mouth. Still, there were people in the rig. He thought he could see a woman's gay-colored dress. Boone gave the bay horse its head and jerked his rawhide reata free. He cut a course that would bring him in behind the team, so as not to turn the runaways altogether too abruptly and upset the rig.

The big bay sensed that this was a race. He needed no quirt or spur to put him to his best. A few minutes of dead running, and Boone was swiftly overhauling the rig. The canvas side curtains had come loose and flapped crazily, shutting the occupants from his sight. Now he was alongside the rig. The rawhide rope swung in a few easy circles, spread in a wide loop, settled over the heads of both mules. Boone jerked the noose tight, then slowly, gradually, pulled the racing team down, pawing and kicking and jerking, to a halt. Their heads noosed together, they stood, legs widespread, sweaty sides heaving. Boone reached from the saddle and picked up the lines that trailed on the ground. Then, for the first time, he looked at the occupants of the army hack.

Lieutenant Clanton, his handsome face ashy gray, was sitting with braced legs, his good arm around Virginia Lee. The girl, pale, wide-eyed with fear, sat stunned for a moment. Then she jerked free from the lieutenant's arm and leaped to the ground. She was trembling a little and crimson spots showed in her cheeks. Lieutenant

Clanton avoided her eyes. He climbed down to the ground. Without a word, Boone handed him the lines.

"I reckon all the run is took out of 'em," said Boone stiffly, jerking his rope free, "but both singletrees is kicked to pieces. Looks like yo're afoot, till help comes. And yonder it comes down the road. It's a freight outfit. Slow but sure travelin', lieutenant."

Lieutenant Clanton flushed angrily. Boone, his self-consciousness suddenly vanished, grinned. He wanted to hurt this girl who had made him feel so deeply hurt. And he wanted to humiliate this uniformed dude who had treated him shabbily.

"You handle a team like you ride," he drawled. "You must belong to the infantry."

"You have me at a disadvantage," said the lieutenant hotly. "I certainly hope we meet again some day, Mister Horse Thief, when my shoulder is healed."

"That goes double," said Boone, coiling his rawhide reata and dropping it across his saddle horn. He lifted his hat.

"I reckon that freight outfit will get you into Miles City by noon, ma'am. Adios." He swung the big bay around.

"Please!" cried the girl. "Just a minute, won't you, please?"

"Yes, ma'am?" Boone pulled up, sitting sideways in his saddle. Virginia Lee stepped over to his horse.

"I came to town this morning with my daddy to thank you. I was so confused last night that I was so rude as to go away without doing so. And now I owe you more thanks. You have put me deeply in your debt. And since Lieutenant Clanton seems to have forgotten that an army officer is supposed to be a gentleman, I will also thank you in his behalf for doing what you did. Won't you please shake hands?"

Boone's self-possession ebbed. He reached from his saddle and his heart pounded like a trip hammer at the pressure of her fingers.

"I — I'd be proud to loan you my horse," he told her, "but he's a one-man horse. I've learned — taught him to be that a way."

"Thanks, but I'd like to ride into town on the freight wagon, I like to hear freighters, when they handle a string team. They cuss so artistically. It won't be the first freight wagon I've ridden. Good-bye, Mr. Boone, and I hope we meet again some day. If you ever get to Fort Benton, please hunt us up. Daddy wants to see you about going out on our ranch. He was terribly disappointed when he learned you'd left town. But I overheard daddy and the sheriff talking and you're going to the Ken Hanley ranch. They're our neighbours on the Teton. I'll be looking forward to seeing you there. Good-bye."

"So long," said Boone, happier than he had ever hoped to be as he looked down into Virginia's eyes.

He rode away with his chin held high and his hat in his hand. As he topped a ridge before dropping into a coulee, he looked back and waved his hat. There came the flutter of a handkerchief in reply.

Back at the disabled rig, Virginia Lee faced Lieutenant Clanton with eyes that no longer smiled.

"I didn't know that an army officer could be such a cad, Lieutenant Clanton. Overlooking the fact that you tried to make one-armed love to me and caused this mess, you lack the decency to thank that cowboy for doing a generous and brave thing. I'm going in on the freight wagon. I'll leave you with your mules."

"Your handsome cowboy," said the white-lipped lieutenant, stung beyond the limit of discretion, "is nothing but a common horse thief. He's riding a horse he stole from me at Fort Whipple."

"I'll have to ask you to prove that, Lieutenant Clanton."

"By gad, I will prove it! And I'll put the thief where he belongs!"

Head tilted, the angry girl walked away. Lieutenant Clanton, his lips bloodless, stood there holding the lines, helpless, raging, already feeling the first pang of regret for the words he had spoken. His shoulder throbbed with pain. He cursed Boone for a horse-stealing nobody who was trying to edge into the good graces of the Lees. And with a grim sort of fury, he decided to carry out his threat to expose Boone for a horse thief. He had made an issue of it. And he salved his conscience with the thought that it was his duty to Virginia and her father to attend to this cowboy.

The mules tugged at the lines, reminding him of his undignified and embarrassing situation. He saw Virginia talking to the freighter. Boiling with rage, he unhooked the mules and tied them to the rig. Then he struck out on foot for town. And as he walked, he planned his campaign against the handsome young cowboy who had humiliated him twice.

Chapter 12

Fort Benton

Head of navigation on the Missouri River, Fort Benton, Montana. Probably the oldest town in the State, and in many ways the most colorful. For it was here that the East met the West, the North met the South. For those coming up the river on the big side-wheel steamers, it was the starting point to romance and high adventure.

Huge piles of hides and bales of furs filled the warehouses there on the river bank. Steamboats unloaded their passengers and took on their cargo of hides and fur pelts. Tenderfeet rubbed elbows with buckskin-garbed trappers and stolid Indians wrapped in their gay blankets. Bull-whackers and mule skinners, their whips cracking like pistol shots, wagon wheels creaking, chains rattling, pulled up and unloaded. Loaded again with supplies for towns far distant, pulled out again.

Cowboys rode the streets. Stores and saloons and gambling halls were packed with all manner of men. Traders, trappers, cow-boys, Indians, gold seekers, tinhorn gam-blers, freighters, half-breeds from the North, soldiers, pioneers with their fami-lies, rivermen, as well as adventurers of all kinds.

Such was Fort Benton, there among the giant cottonwoods, that day when Boone rode into the town. To him it was the real-ization of a dream. Here was a glimpse of the muddy river Jawbone had so often spoken of, with its great boats. Here was life, painted in all of its colors.

Boone stabled his horse and spent the rest of the day walking around the town. He sat on the bank of the river and watched a big side-wheeler dock. With eyes alight with excitement, he saw the crowd of passengers come ashore. Color and laughter and shouts. Buckskin and broadcloth, faded flannel and gay-colored silks. Bearded men. Bonneted women. The leafy cottonwoods splashing the sunlit water with shadows. A blue sky spotted with woolly white clouds. Boone sat apart from the crowd and watched with the eyes of a dreamer. And as he watched he kept thinking that this was Virginia Lee's town. She was a part of this life. She belonged among those people yonder who had come, in carriages, to watch the docking of the river boat. Men in white linen and black broadcloth. Women in flowered dresses, carrying parasols. They laughed a lot, those people in their carriages.

A sadness clouded Boone's eyes until their gray seemed almost black. It was the gay laughter of those people yonder that made Boone feel shut off and alone, because he had never known how to laugh. It was as if that laughter formed a barrier between him and them. More than their wealth, their education, their fine clothes, their laughter symbolized that which they were and which he was not. Life had cheated him out of that which they had without being conscious of possessing.

He got to his feet and walked slowly back uptown. His clothes were weather-worn and patched. His boots needed mending. His hat was shapeless. He was badly in need of a shave and a haircut. He had given his last coins to the man who owned the feed barn. He was hungry and without the price to buy a meal or a bed. Yet he walked with his head held high, his shoulders straight, with that stiff-legged gait of a man more at home on horseback than on the ground.

In his pocket was that letter from Sheriff

Bill Hanley to his brother on the Teton. Ken Hanley's ranch joined the Lee place. Virginia Lee belonged with those people in their carriages. The people who knew how to laugh —

Boone halted beside a fire where some Indians were cooking. He took the letter from his pocket and tossed it into the flames. He stood there, heedless of the curious eyes of the Indians, and watched the letter burn. Then he walked on.

Down the crowded street that teemed with life. Past the open doorways of stores and saloons and restaurants and barber shops. Drifting along with the crowd, yet not one of them. A stranger in a strange land that had, at first, seemed his trail's end. Now it was but another brief stopping place on his restless search for something to which he could not give a name.

At first, so wrapped in his thoughts was Boone, he did not recognize the bearded, flashily dressed man who blocked his way, with a crooked grin on his face and eyes red-shot from whisky fumes. The man was holding out a grimy hand on which shone a big diamond ring.

"Ain't you gonna shake with your ol' pardner, young un?"

"Jawbone!" Rudely jerked from his

thoughts, Boone stared at the overdressed renegade who swayed a little unsteadily on his feet. Boone made no move to take the proffered hand, and Jawbone laughed gratingly.

"High-toned, are you? Well, many's the rooster as crowed of a mornin' got his head nicked off afore dark. You think you ain't fit to herd with my kind. Well, that suits me all right. You're a-wearin' rags and I'm a-wearin' diamonds."

"And if you don't be careful," said Boone, "you'll be wearin' a rope tied around your neck. You and me split the blankets back there in Wyoming."

Jawbone hung his thumbs in the armholes of his plaid vest, which was spotted with tobacco stains and spilled liquor. His slitted, bloodshot eyes were kindled with a dangerous light, cunning, calculating, cruel. Under each armpit, in tied holsters, reposed a big Colt gun. For a moment, Boone thought the renegade was planning a gun play, and his own hand dropped to the cedar butt of the gun strapped to his thigh. Then Jawbone's coarse-lipped mouth twisted as he roughly croaked:

"I'm rich, young un. Money in every pocket and diamonds on my fingers. There's plenty more money where this come from. And if you had a lick of sense, I'd take you back for a pardner's share. Yo're broke, and don't deny it. Better throw in with ol' Jawbone and get your share."

"You foller your trail, Jawbone, and leave me alone. I used to be a-scared of you, but I ain't scared any more. Foller your trail. I'll foller mine, I'm done with you."

"Are you, now? I ain't so positive about that, young un. I didn't spend them years raisin' you from a pup just because I liked young brats. Now yo're worth big money to me, and I'll get back what it cost me to raise you. You ain't givin' ol' Jawbone the slip again. I'll make money off you or I'll kill you, one." With a mocking bow that was a trifle wobbly, Jawbone stepped aside to let the boy pass.

Boone walked on alone, while Jawbone stood there on the plank sidewalk, looking after the boy, an evil grin on his face. Then, when Boone was lost in the crowd, the renegade pushed his way into the nearest saloon. A man who had been standing outside followed him in and took place alongside him at the bar.

"Is that the young un, pardner?"

"That's our huckleberry, Pete. He's worth more than a placer mine."

"I'm doggoned if I see how he's worth a dime to us."

"That," leered Jawbone, "is for me to know and you find out later. Did 'Big Nose' trail him?"

"Shore thing."

Jawbone grinned and lifted his whisky. "Here's luck."

Chapter 13

Jeremy Lee

His pockets empty, Boone walked aimlessly on. Meeting Jawbone had upset him. And the meeting had further brought home to him the gulf that separated him from the beautiful daughter of Judge Lee. He drifted along. There was a large crowd gathered down on the river bank. Boone, for want of something better to do, joined the throng.

A river gambler and a tipsy man in buckskin were shooting with pistols at a mark, this being a white block of wood tossed into the river. The swirling current carried it along, spinning it in small whirlpools, bearing it downstream. In turn, both men emptied their pistols at the mark. Neither man hit the bobbing target. A ribald laugh went up from the crowd. This angered both contestants, and the man in the fringed buckskin, with much profanity, challenged any man in the crowd to hit the elusive target. Immediately a dozen pistols cracked. Jets of water spurted around the little block of wood. Only one of the bullets came close enough to resemble good shooting. Most of the crowd were tenderfeet.

"I'll bet any man here a hundred dollars," said the river gambler, "that he can't hit it."

"Call the bet!"

Boone's long-barrelled gun slid out. In rapid succession, so close together that it was like the roll of a drumbeat, Boone poured hot lead at the little block, lifting it from the water. Every shot hit the block. A cheer went up from the crowd. With a ready hand the gambler paid Boone the hundred dollars. The buckskin-clad man grinned his admiration.

"That," said the river gambler, "is real shooting. I feel a great sorrow for the man who engages you in a gun-throwing argument."

Boone smiled and reloaded his gun. "It's just practice," he said, "and mebbe so a knack for handlin' guns. Just like some run to cards or foot racin'."

The tipsy man in buckskin slapped Boone on the back. "Ye showed us up, no mistake about that. I'd buy a drink for you."

Boone shook his head. "A big steak and

potatoes is more to my likin'."

"In which case," said the gambler, "I'd be honoured to have you join me at supper. I think I can make us both a little odd change."

The gambler was a man in his early thirties, well dressed and soft spoken. A black-haired, black-moustached, black-eyed man with a handsome face the color of ivory. He had a polish and easy flow of words that made Boone envy him. He took Boone's arm and together they went back uptown.

The gambler led the way into a restaurant run by a Chinaman. With a smile and a gesture, the gambler seated Boone at an empty table, situated in an obscure corner of the place. Boone sat down. Then, to the gambler's surprise, he shoved the hundred dollars across the table.

"I'll have supper with you," said Boone, "but I don't feel like I could take your money. You see, I was broke. If I'd lost, I couldn't have paid off what I owed."

The gambler smiled. "It is a pleasure to meet a man of honor." His slim fingers divided the money. "Fifty for you. Fifty for me. And when we've done justice to this meal, we'll talk business. Frankly speaking, that was my last hundred. I'd planned to win something from our friend in the soiled buckskins, but as you see, I failed. Every man to his own game. I never could shoot well. But I figured that our buckskin fellow was even worse than I. Are you acquainted around here, friend?"

"I just got in to-day."

"So did I. Came up on the boat from St. Louis. And lost what I had to wiser and more accomplished card shufflers. . . . I wonder what your partner wants?"

"Pardner?" Boone shook his head. "I haven't any pardner."

"Then you don't know the hairy fellow sitting at that table yonder? The chap with the oversized nose?"

Boone followed the direction of the gambler's glance. He saw a bearded, roughly clad man sitting at a table near by, drinking raw whisky. The man's eyes dropped as Boone looked his way.

"Never saw him before," said Boone.

"He followed you down to the river. He followed us here."

The man with the big nose finished his whisky and slouched out without a backward glance. Boone's eyes followed him through the door.

Just as the man passed into the dusk, from outside came the crack of a gun. The

big-nosed man took a faltering step backward, his gun spewing flame as he fired
from the hip. Then he crumpled in a heap.

Boone ran to where the man lay. The
bearded fellow, red gushing from his
mouth, looked at the boy with glazing eyes.

"Harmer," he whispered, as Boone lifted
his head. "Tell Jawbone that . . . Tex
Harmer's ketched up. . . ."

The bearded head dropped limply. The
man was dead. Boone glanced up, to see
the river gambler eyeing him smilingly.

A crowd gathered. A man with a deputy
sheriff's badge had the dead man carried
away. There seemed to be no one who had
seen the man who had been victor in the
swift duel.

The river gambler led Boone back to the
table. The gambler was calm of manner,
smiling faintly, his black eyes opaque.

"Queer proposition, life. A minute ago
the big-nosed party sat there enjoying his
drink. Now he's dead. He's gone across the
black river. A godless, hard-living man,
judging him by his looks. He died without
thinking of what lay in wait for him on
yonder side of that black river. Without an
effort at atonement, without a chance to
balance his account here on earth. Just
pitched his last chips into the jackpot, lay

down a losing hand, and pushed back his chair. Alive today, dead tomorrow." He called the Chinaman and ordered two drinks.

"To bring back our appetites," he explained. "By the way, my name is Lee, Jeremy Lee. And yours?"

"Boone."

"Boone? By Jove, that's an odd one!"

"Odd one?" inquired Boone, puzzled.

"Beg pardon, sir," smiled the gambler, "I was musing aloud. The name of Boone recalled a bit of history. . . . Family history. It's of no importance here." He lifted the drink at his elbow. "To our further acquaintance, Mr. Boone," and, as their glasses touched, "I would like to add, to a future friendship!"

"Thanks. The same to you, sir." They drank.

"And now, friend Boone," said the gambler, "I'd like to team with you for a while. With my promotion, and your skill as a marksman, we might line our pockets with something besides lint. Like our friend in the soiled buckskins, many of these gents are of the opinion that they can shoot. I'll handle the situation up to the point where they are inclined to back their skill with gold. Then you step up, beat them at the game, and we divide the profits. It's no swindle. There may be times when we'll lose. The boat leaves to-morrow morning, going down the river. It will have a passenger list that will contain men who have money they've made here. And as we float down the river, we will arrange these little pistol matches. I'd intended staying here, but due to the fact that I am not financially strong, I'll be leaving on the next boat. After supper, I'll run my fifty dollars up to a sum sufficient to pay our passage. You could use your fifty to purchase some of the things you need in the way of clothes. Though I've plenty for us both and we're near enough of a size to use the same wardrobe. Would you care for the partnership?"

"I'd like to go down the river," said Boone, "and I don't feel like stayin' here at Fort Benton. I'll go with you."

"That's the sporting instinct, Boone. Shake on it."

The Chinaman brought their food. After supper, Boone and his companion strolled around. Boone wanted to see that his horse was being well cared for, so they went down to the barn. Boone kept thinking of that big-nosed man who had spoken of Tex Harmer and Jawbone. The man who had followed him. The man whom Tex Harmer had shot down.

Boone walked with his eyes searching the faces of the men they met. Once he thought he saw Jawbone. And another time he was almost certain that he caught a glimpse of Tex Harmer's sinister face in the crowd. Boone's hand stayed near his gun, a fact which the gambler didn't miss.

On the way to the barn, Boone spoke of Judge Lee. The gambler smiled and nodded.

"My uncle. I came up the river with a letter to him. It was my father's notion that I study law under the judge. But law is a musty calling and drained of all adventure or romance. I couldn't be stuffed into an office lined with books, Boone. Not when there's romance and adventure waiting. So I chucked the letter in the river and made up my mind to hunt my own life's trail. I thought I'd look up my uncle and my cousin here, but they're not at home. So we'll win a stake tonight and set out on the trail to adventure. Kismet. Fate. A Boone and a Lee. And we sit on the lap of the gods."

There was a reckless gaity in Jeremy Lee's bearing. His dark eyes flashed and there was a dangerous ring to his voice when he spoke his dreams aloud. His laugh was easy, his manner polished. Unconsciously, Boone absorbed much of his manner of speaking and bearing. For here was a young man who belonged with those people who rode in fine carriages, yet put aside that life to mingle with gamblers and men below his standard of refinement and education. Here was a true adventurer, a soldier of fortune.

Jeremy Lee knew horses. And when he saw Boone's splendid bay gelding, he showed him the points of the horse that indicated a well-bred piece of horseflesh.

"What will you do with him while you're gone, Boone?"

"I'll be hanged if I know," admitted Boone.

"My uncle has a ranch near here. Why not ride him out there and leave him? I'll write a letter to the judge, saying a friend of mine is leaving his horse for an indefinite period."

"I reckon I'd better write the letter," said Boone. "I've met Judge Lee and I reckon he'd be willin' to take care of my horse for me."

"Then ride out there and leave the horse. Then come on back, get barbered and bathed and into my clothes. And meet me at breakfast. I'll have passage money for us. We'll go part way down the river, or all the way, perhaps. And I'll show you St. Louis."

His arm was across Boone's shoulders in a gesture of comradeship that made Boone forget something of the bitterness in his heart.

"If you could teach me something of books and decent manners," said Boone, "and help me to be something besides a common cowhand, I'd do anything to earn my way along."

"You've struck a bargain, Boone. We'll see life together you and I. Now, saddle up and get out there and back. Borrow a horse to come back on. Don't look for me until breakfast time. Here's the key to my room at the hotel. Help yourself to what you want out of my trunk. Wish me luck in the night's card. And — au revoir."

With a gay wave of his hand, Jeremy Lee swaggered away. Boone saddled Get-away and hired another horse to lead out to the Lee ranch. As he left the barn, he thought he saw a man dodge behind some wagons. But the light was uncertain and he could not be positive. He inquired the way to the Lee ranch on the Teton, then hit a swift trot.

It was almost midnight when he reached

the Lee ranch. At the bunk house, he succeeded in rousing the foreman. Much to Boone's glad surprise, there were two cow punchers there who had been with the SL herd coming up the trail. They greeted Boone warmly and wanted him to stay all night. But he evaded the hearty invitation and left the big bay horse in the barn.

"So long, Get-away, old man. I'll be seein' you again." Parting with the big bay gelding put a lump in the boy's throat. He left the ranch with the feeling that he had left a friend. At Fort Benton the same night, or rather early next morning, he sat in Jeremy Lee's room and composed a letter to Virginia Lee. In it he told her he was giving her the bay horse to keep until he returned some day. Or if he did not return, the horse was hers. That, with good treatment and patience, the big bay would understand her and let her do anything with him.

Boone said no word about her cousin Jeremy. Nor did he mention where he was going, or why. He simply promised to come back some day when he had accomplished something that had to be done.

He mailed the letter at the post office and was on his way back to the hotel when a man stepped out of the darkness, a drawn gun in his hand.

"You killed Big Nose, but now it's your turn! And if Jawbone don't like it, I'll send him after you!"

The man was drunk. His voice, thick with anger, was deadly. With a quick leap sideways, Boone was on top of the man. He felt the powder burn his cheek as the man jerked the trigger. Then Boone's big Colt thudded against the man's jaw, staggering him. Again the gun barrel crashed against bone, and the man wilted. Some one was coming at a run. Boone ducked back into the shadow, around a building, and into a gambling place. He slowed his pace and walked with well-feigned carelessness up to the bar. He was wondering how many more of Jawbone's friends he would encounter, if luck would let him get out of Fort Benton alive and without killing someone.

He looked through the crowd. Not a familiar face in the throng that milled around the tables. Boone could understand how Jawbone might come to decide that he had killed Big Nose. Because the boy was positive now that Big Nose had been following him. Nobody had seen the killing, and Jawbone was certainly not hunting up the deputy sheriff to ask questions. Jawbone hated law officers with a wholehearted hatred that was venomous.

More on his guard than ever, Boone loafed around the gambling hall and saloon. He took care to watch the doors and not to turn his back on any man who looked at all suspicious. And he was wishing he could find Jeremy Lee. He had taken a strong liking to the handsome river gambler. And he knew, in spite of the fact that the card shuffler sometimes looked at him with a sort of sardonic suspicion, that the liking was mutual. Plainly, Jeremy Lee figured that Boone was connected with some sort of shady dealings. He had heard the dying words the big-nosed outlaw spoke.

It was still an hour or so until daylight. The gambling and drinking were going full blast. Those of lesser capacity had staggered away to sleep off their jags. One of the gambling games had been going for two days and nights, so the bartender told Boone. It was a big game, between a cowman and a mining man. Others dropping in for a few hours to lose or win, then go away. The two real gamblers betting high with chips worth a hundred dollars apiece. It would end, so Boone was told, in either one or the other of the men losing all he had. Either the mine or the cattle ranch would change hands before the two quit playing.

One of the stud dealers was a Chinaman whose long queue was coiled under a round black skullcap. He was one of the most popular dealers, and reputed to be very wealthy.

Boone finally tired of watching the playing and decided to wait for Jeremy Lee at the hotel. So he returned to the room. Lighting the lamp, he gave a grunt of astonishment.

The orderly room he had left but an hour or so ago was now in wild disorder. Clothes strewed the place, their pockets inside out. There was every indication that some one had, intent on robbery, ransacked the room. Even the bedclothes and carpet had been searched. The burglars had made no attempt at secrecy.

Chapter 14

Cowboy and Wanderer

As Boone was straightening up the place the door opened to admit Jeremy Lee. The gambler surveyed the disorder with no change of expression save for the knowing lift of an eyebrow.

"Somebody went through your stuff," said Boone.

The river gambler nodded. "These folks get intimate of rather short acquaintance. Well, they got nothing of any value. Don't take it so seriously, friend."

Jeremy Lee produced a silver-and-leather-embossed flask and poured a drink into a small silver cup that served as a screw top for the ornate container.

"Drink, Boone?"

"No thanks."

"I've waited all night for this one. Never touch it when I'm working." He tossed off the drink, followed it with another, then put the flask back in his pocket. He removed his tailored coat and took two pistols from their scabbards. Then he dropped several stacks of bank notes into his beaver hat.

"I'm afraid our trip down the river will have to wait, friend. Just how long a delay, I can't tell as yet." Picking up the tall-crowned hat, he poked a finger through a hole on the crown. His lips smiled under the trimmed black moustache, but his black eyes glittered dangerously.

"I'd venture to say that the coward who tried to pot me from the dark to-night is somehow connected with this bit of bur-glary. You have not told any one my name, have you, friend? Or that I am Judge Lee's nephew?"

"I haven't told a soul."

"Did you, by any chance, deliver the odd message given you by that big-nosed man who spoiled our dinner by being killed?" Jeremy Lee's eyes searched Boone's face.

"No, I didn't deliver the message. I haven't seen Jawbone Smith."

"But you did see a man known as 'White Pete'?"

"Never heard of him."

"Perhaps not. He's laid up with a cracked head and a broken jaw. From the few words I overheard spoken, I judged you were the cause of the gentleman's misfortune. Perhaps they were referring to another man named Boone."

"A gent tried to kill me," said Boone, "and I knocked him down with my gun. I don't know what his name is. I don't know what he looks like. But he had some fool idea that it was me that killed that big-nosed gent."

"I judged as much from what I overheard. It might be wise for you to convey that death message given you by the party with the bulbous beak. It might change the direction of the bullets that they throw about in such a prodigal manner."

"If Tex Harmer killed that gent," said Boone, "it won't be long until Harmer and Jawbone locks horns. And if they both die, so much the better. Because either of 'em would kill me if they got the right chance."

"For a young man," said Jeremy Lee, "you have acquired a number of dangerous enemies." Humming a gay tune, the river gambler stripped off his clothes and took a cold bath. Then he shaved. Now and then he addressed some trivial remark to Boone, who sat in a chair, unshaven, still in his rough clothes. Boone sensed a subtle change in the gambler's manner toward him. Jeremy Lee had not yet said why he had changed his plans about going down the river, and Boone could not keep from wondering what had happened.

It occurred to Boone that perhaps he had thought better of taking as a partner such a shabby, uncouth, and penniless man as he. Then, there was that matter of the bullet hole in Lee's hat. Who had shot that bullet? Jawbone or one of his cronies?

"Did you get a look at the man that shot at you, Lee?" he finally asked.

"No. But I'll find him. And when I do, I'll try to shoot better than you saw me shoot at the target on the river. That hat cost me fifty dollars in New Orleans."

"Mebbe," said Boone, "it was one of those gents that don't like me. And because you were seen with me, they're includin' you in their grudge."

"I wondered as much," nodded the gambler.

"In which case, I better go my own trail alone," said Boone. "I ain't sharin' my troubles with any man."

Jeremy Lee, who sat on the edge of the disordered bed pulling on his polished boots, looked up and smiled thinly.

"It might be better, Boone, if we did part company for the present. You see, I've changed my mind about going down the river. I think I will hunt up my uncle's partner in the law firm and commence burrowing into the musty books. I won enough tonight to line my pockets and salve my self-respect. Had a run of luck. Ran that fifty up to three thousand and some odd hundred dollars. Help yourself to what you need."

"I don't need a dollar of it," said Boone.

"But you need money, friend. And there's plenty there in the hat. Consider it a loan till you get on your feet again."

Boone shook his head. "I reckon not, thanks. I wouldn't feel right about it."

"I can understand, Boone, how you feel. Suit yourself. But you're welcome to take what you want. You've brought me luck."

Boone held out his hand.

"Mebbe I'll be seein' you."

"If you stay in Fort Benton," said the gambler, taking Boone's hand, "you will. Sorry we lost out on the river trip."

There was a decided coolness to Jeremy Lee's manner that stung Boone to the quick. He could not fathom the gambler, whose smile had no meaning and whose eyes were opaque, unreadable. He left the room quickly and went downstairs. It was daylight now. A few men were in the hotel office. Boone passed on outside.

To him it seemed that fate was kicking

him around a lot. Promising things, then taking them away before he could grip them. Giving him glimpses of hope, then darkening the rays of its sunshine. Jeremy Lee's actions were puzzling, confusing, and irritating. At first the man had been so cordial of manner, so frank and friendly. Now he had turned cold, almost suspicious. Well, perhaps gamblers were like that. Suspicious of all men. But still, there must have been some strong cause for that quick change from friendliness to coldness.

Boone turned into the open doorway of a saloon and gambling place. His hand, inside his pocket, gripped the fifty dollars he had gotten from Jeremy Lee the day before as the result of a wager. In a way, it belonged to him, but the feel of it in his pocket was uncomfortable.

Even at this hour before sunrise, the gambling layouts were being well patronized. Boone stepped to the roulette wheel and after watching the play for a few spins of the wheel, laid his money down on a number. He knew little of gambling. He had no instinct for cards, or dice, or the wheel.

The wheel spun dizzily, slowed, the small white ball racing its circular course. It fell into one of the numbered notches. The gambler began collecting his winnings. Boone was about to turn away when, with a start, he saw the man paying. Boone, who had placed his money there to lose it, had won.

For more than an hour, Boone played, not caring whether he won or lost. Gold and bank notes piled in front of him. The man with the weary eyes who spun the wheel called for more house money. A crowd gathered about the shabby, unshorn cowboy who was winning. Two hours later Boone quit the table. His pockets were stuffed with money, the first money he had ever won gambling.

Boone did not know how much money he had won. But he was richer than he had ever been in his life. Gold sagged the pockets of his shabby clothes. Greenbacks bulged in wads in every pocket. He was rich. Dazed, he walked to the bar and ordered a drink. After the custom, he called every man up to the bar. Where he had been friendless a few hours before, he now had a host of men eager to become his friends. Boone lifted his glass.

"Here's how!" He drank, then pushed out through the crowd without waiting for his change. He wanted to breathe fresh air that was untainted by stale tobacco smoke and liquor fumes. He sought a barber shop where a sign told him that a shave cost a dollar, a haircut two dollars, baths fifty cents. On his way to the barber shop he stopped at a store and bought some clothes.

Some time later Boone emerged, shaved, bathed, dressed in clean garments. He felt more like a man, now. He hunted up the law office of Lee & Lorrimer, attorneys at law, and there left a bulky envelope to be delivered to Jeremy Lee. The clerk said that Jeremy Lee had not yet put in an appearance but that they expected him. Boone then left the office and went to the hotel. He had left fifty dollars there for the gambler.

That, he reflected, not without a little bitterness, paid off his debt to Jeremy Lee, river gambler and nephew of Judge Lee. And, by the same token, cousin of Virginia Lee, who belonged in a world that shut out such as Boone, cowboy and wanderer.

Chapter 15

Defiance

Determined to buy passage on one of the big boats going down the river, Boone strolled down that way. It was a cloudless morning and all was bustle and hurry. The streets teemed with life, life that was crude and earthy and flavored with adventure.

A big white stern-wheeler was coming up the river, its whistle pulled open, its deck swarming with people. And on the bank a large throng gathered to greet the boat. Now, as Boone walked that direction, a carriage passed. It was drawn by a handsome pair of sleek blacks. And beside its driver, it held two occupants. One of the two, Boone recognized as Jeremy Lee. The man with him was none other than Lieutenant Harry Clanton. They were talking and laughing and neither of them took notice of Boone as the carriage rolled past him.

The boat was docking now. The gangplank was let down. A band played. The passengers were coming ashore. Boone found himself wedged in the crowd that pushed and jostled one another with good-natured eagerness. Boone caught a brief glimpse of Jawbone up ahead. Then the crowd came between them. He saw Jeremy Lee and Lieutenant Clanton standing up on the driver's seat of the open carriage, scanning the crowd. Now, across the crowd, Boone's gaze met Lieutenant Clanton's and the latter nudged the gambler and pointed. Jeremy Lee looked at Boone with- out a trace of recognition. Boone's face grew hot with anger. He could imagine the army man saying that Boone was a horse thief and a partner of the unsavoury Jawbone.

Now there came a confusion up ahead in the crowd. Voices raised in anger. A shouted order. A pistol shot. The terrified scream of a woman. The splash of a man leaping into the river. Boone was caught in the rush, carried along, stumbling and twisting. Now the crowd opened. A man lay on the ground his head pillowed in a woman's lap. With a sharp cry, Boone pushed forward. The woman looked up, her white face stricken with terror and grief. It was Virginia Lee, and the man who lay, so white and still, red staining his white shirt front, was her father, Judge Lee.

"Gangway, there!" Lieutenant Clanton and Jeremy Lee smashed through the crowd. Clanton pointed at Boone, who now knelt beside the wounded judge.

"Seize that man, in the name of the law!" shouted the army officer.

"He didn't do it!" called someone.

"His partner did!" barked Clanton. "Grab him!"

The next moment rough, strong hands seized Boone and held him. A rope was bound around his arms. The crowd, incensed at the shooting of the prominent and popular judge, surged curiously around the white-lipped prisoner.

"Lynch him!" ran the cries. "String him up! Where's a rope?"

Boone fought in a futile effort to free his arms. Lieutenant Clanton and Jeremy Lee were carrying the wounded and unconscious judge to their carriage. A mob of citizens were crowding the bank, hunting for the would-be murderer who had dived into the muddy water. Men were shooting at any floating object that might resemble the head of a swimming man.

Now Jeremy Lee fought his way back into the crowd, as they bore Boone away toward the cottonwoods. There was a noose around Boone's neck.

Boone sought the faces of the mob for a friend. He smiled faintly as he recognized the prime leader of the mob. The leader was Tex Harmer and pinned to his shirt was a law-officer's star.

Now Jeremy Lee, beating his way through the mob, stood beside Boone. The gambler jerked the rope from around the prisoner's neck.

"Hold on, men! If he's guilty, he'll be punished. But he'll not be strung up this way. I'm Judge Lee's nephew and I'll be responsible."

Now came a shout from the river bank. Men were pointing to the swirling water. Pistols popped.

"Yonder he swims! There he is! Near the other shore! Fetch a rifle!" Tex Harmer's voice saying, "He's Jawbone Smith, wanted for murder."

Jeremy Lee turned to Boone with a sardonic smile.

"Here," he said in a brittle voice, "is your chance for freedom, friend." He shoved Boone to the river's edge. Boone felt the rope that bound his arms cut apart. With a thin smile the river gambler handed Boone one of his long-barrelled pistols. The companion to it was in Jeremy Lee's hand.

"If you shoot as well, my friend, as you shot at the target, you'll kill the yellow coward that shot Judge Lee. Try to escape and I'll plug you. Stand back, men. Give the marksman elbow room!"

Boone balanced the pistol in his hand. It was a splendid weapon, built for accurate shooting. Yonder, swimming desperately down current, angling for the opposite bank, swam the man whom Boone now knew to be Jawbone. The range was a little far for the average pistol shot. But with reasonable luck, Boone could hit the moving target.

"Kill him," said the river gambler coldly, "and you may stand a chance to clear yourself of being a party to this conspiracy to assassinate a real man."

For a moment Boone stood there, balancing the gun, his eyes puckered a little at the corners. In that moment his thoughts raced swiftly. His resentment toward this unwarranted condemnation seared his brain like a white-hot iron. With a bitter smile he handed the gun, butt foremost, to the nephew of Judge Lee.

"I have done no wrong and I'll stand my hand. Here's your gun, Mister Jeremy Lee. Do your own killing."

Head lifted, his grey, black-flecked eyes

blazing with anger and defiance, Boone faced Jeremy Lee and the crowd.

Now the sheriff and some deputies came up. Handcuff were snapped on Boone's wrists. As he was being led away he saw Jawbone's head, a black spot on the yellow water, water that was bullet-sprayed, drop entirely from sight. Whether he had been hit or whether he had dived under the surface to come up again in the shelter of the willows that grew in the water by the river bank, no man could tell.

Chapter 16

"Shake Yo' Feet, Cowboy"

At the jail, Boone was searched. The money he had won was counted before him and placed in a sealed envelope. There had been eighteen hundred dollars in the total sum. Jeremy Lee was there, watching it being counted. He looked at Boone with his opaque, black eyes.

"Last I saw of you, friend, you had about fifty dollars. Your erstwhile companion Jawbone, and his partners, are suspected of being engaged in all sorts of thievery ranging from burglary to highway robbery. You might have trouble explaining this sudden wealth."

"I won it gambling. I can prove it by the gambler that runs the roulette wheel at the Gold Bug Saloon. A thin-faced gent they call 'Dude.' Dude King, I think."

"Dude King," said a deputy, "left on the boat that just pulled out."

Jeremy Lee turned and walked away, whistling in an almost inaudible tone.

Boone was taken to a cell that already held one occupant, a Negro army deserter.

"If Judge Lee dies," said the sheriff grimly, "I reckon you'll be tried for murder. As things stand, yo're up against a horse-stealin' charge brought against you by Lieutenant Harry Clanton. For a young man, you've sure travelled hard and loose. You don't look that ornery."

"You never can tell," said Boone, forcing a smile, "by the length of a frog's legs, how far he can jump. Better keep an eye on me, mister. I might get to chawin' these iron bars off with my teeth."

"Yo're a heap safer here in jail than you'd be runnin' loose. There's a lot of talk about lynchin', uptown."

"And I reckon that Tex Harmer might be able to tell you who is ribbin' this necktie party. He wears a nice, shiny badge that he hides behind."

"He's trailing the Red Rock bank robbers. You might be one of 'em, from all reports."

Boone grinned. So much in the way of calamity had fallen on him, that he could almost enjoy the situation.

"If you hear of any women and children and old men and cripples bein' beat up or murdered, sheriff, just add 'em to the list of crimes marked against me."

"Whatever you are, young feller, you ain't a coward. How are you fixed for tobacco and such?"

"I'll get along."

When the sheriff had gone away, the Negro grinned widely.

"Dis heah law sho' bears down hard on a boy, ain't he?"

Boone tossed his dusky cellmate tobacco. And when the man had filled his cob pipe, he brought forth a battered banjo and played on it. His one worry seemed to be if he'd get catfish for supper. Jolly and as friendly as a large puppy, his singing and playing cheered Boone.

"Ah got me friends on de outside. Cowboys like you-all. I bin a-cookin' fer 'em on de ranch. Dey ain't gonna let dis heah boy git de wust of it. Dey aims tuh see dis heah jedge an' buy me outa ol' ahmy fum which ah runs off fum. Yes, suh. No mo' bugles for dis black boy. Ah's a cook. Boss man Till Driscoll likely show up now mos' any day wif my dischahge papehs."

"Till Driscoll?" questioned Boone, the name of the friendly trail boss sending a ray of hope through the blackness. "Where is he now?"

"Deliverin' some cattle at Fort Shaw, on

Sun River. He 'lowed he be back heah some time dis heah week. 'Em law folks step lively den. Ain't nobody fool wid boss-man Till Driscoll when he lose his round-up cook. No, suh."

"I come part way up the trail with Till Driscoll's herd," said Boone. "As far as Red Rock."

"Lawdy, Lawdy, boy, you ain't dis heah Boone boy dey talk about?"

"That's me, or what's left of me."

"Sakes alive, boy, boss-man Till Driscoll bin a-huntin' high an' wide fo' you! He says he got good news. He ain't say what dis good news all about but he sho' frettin' tuh find you-all."

"Well," said Boone, "I won't be hard to locate for a while, accordin' to the sign. If they don't hang me, I'll be here till I'm white-headed. Here or in the big prison."

"Don't you-all go frettin', white boy. Sit yo' se'f down an' smoke till 'at boss-man Till Driscoll show up. He git you outa dis calaboose in no time. Now listen at dis heah jig tune I pick up. Shake yo' feet to dis tune, cowboy."

Chapter 17

Ken Hanley's Visit

But it was Ken Hanley, not Till Driscoll, who was the first to lend a friendly hand to Boone in his predicament. The day after the boy's arrest, Ken Hanley came to visit him.

"Got word from my brother Bill in Miles City that you was comin' to the ranch, son. Next I knowed I get word from Virginia Lee that they're throwed you in jail and that the judge was bad hurt and not expected to live. So Martha and I come to town, right off. Now sit down, my boy, and let's have the yarn from start to finish. If there's anything the sheriff here shouldn't be hearin', I'll send him out."

The sheriff had brought Boone in his office. He had shown the prisoner every decent courtesy. Boone smiled at this big, broad-chested, heavy-voiced cowman whose hand grip had made him wince a little. Here was wholehearted friendship that would weather any sort of storm. His blue eyes twinkled with kindly lights. Here was

145

a man Boone could talk to.

"I shore hate to go whinin' my troubles to folks, sir."

"Whinin', nothin'! They think they got you in tight, and if I'm gonna drag you outa the bog, I want to know the whole story. And it won't hurt the sheriff's ears none to hear the truth. Brother Bill said you was decent and straight as a die, and I've yet to know of any man or horse that he didn't size up right. And that little Virginia gal is sharin' Bill's opinion. And she's no scatterbrain when it comes to readin' a man's brand and earmarks."

"She don't think I had anything to do with the judge bein' shot?"

"Shucks, no. And it'll take more than that purty lieutenant and this nephew of the judge's to turn her mind. Give us the whole gol-darned story."

Boone talked for a long time while the two men listened. Beginning years back as far as he could remember, he told them of his life with Jawbone. Simply, with homely words, without trimmings, he gave them his story. He mentioned Beaver Brown, and Tex Harmer and the parts they had played in his wanderings. Down to the moment on the river bank when he had refused to shoot Jawbone. Because, so he explained simply, he did not think that killing a man who was unable to fight back was the right and proper way to clear his own name of the charges against him. He felt that Jeremy Lee had not acted rightly. That he, Boone, had been condemned without a fair chance. And that Jeremy Lee's friendship was not sincere at the start

"You done right, son," said Ken Hanley. "Yes, sir, you done a man's job of it. For all that he's Judge Lee's nephew, he's not a man I'd care to trust. Few gamblers, to my way of thinkin', can be trusted. And I'm of the opinion that there is more behind this than I first figgered. Will you answer me one question?"

"One or a hundred, sir, if I'm able."

"Your name is Boone. Did you ever hear that Judge Lee once fought a duel with a man named Boone and that Boone was killed by the judge's gun?"

"No, sir. That's the first I ever heard of it."

Ken Hanley nodded, smiling to himself thoughtfully.

"I'll be back later on with a lawyer, Boone. The sheriff will take good care of you. We'll delay the trial just as long as we can. Yep, there's a heap more to this than can be seen with the naked eye. And all you've said is between you and me and the sheriff here. It's a straight story, sheriff, told with a straight tongue. And when they try to harm this boy, they're gonna get hurt some before I'm done with 'em."

He shook hands with Boone and his eyes twinkled brightly.

"I'll give 'Jinny' your message, son."

"But I didn't give you any message."

Ken Hanley's big laugh filled the office. Boone's face was red. The sheriff chuckled. And for some reason Boone felt the sting of unshed tears. But if the men noticed, they paid no attention.

Boone, a lump in his throat, was taken back to his cell, where the Negro was crooning a folk song to the accompaniment of his battered old banjo.

Boone thought that the cell was less dark than it had been, and that the songs of his companion were sweeter and more plaintive than ever. From the small, barred window Boone could see the river with its boats, its green banks, its huge cottonwoods. And on the other side, a high, yellowish clay-cut bank. Even the drab clay and the muddy water looked beautiful to the boy as he stood there, looking out.

Ken Hanley's visit had cheered Boone. He was ready to face whatever lay ahead of him if Ken Hanley and Virginia Lee believed in him. It seemed incredible that such a beautiful girl, educated, rich, refined, could care one way or another about a tramp cowboy of unknown origin.

But perhaps she was only doing that much because her heart was kind, in the same way that she might feed a stray dog. Boone was afraid to hope for much. Every dream he had ever built had tumbled in ruins. But still and all, it was mighty good to know that she didn't condemn him. Even when it was her own father who lay in the hospital badly wounded, perhaps dying.

He wondered why Jawbone had shot Judge Lee. And he wondered if there was any connection between himself and the Boone who had fallen in a duel fought with the now famous jurist. And if this attempted assassination had aught to do with the duel and with himself.

The jail window was open. Only the iron bars separated Boone from freedom. Now, as he stood there, a man shambled past. A man in greasy buckskins, with scraggly hair and beard. From under a battered hat a pair of fox-like eyes shifted their gaze upward. Boone was on the point of calling out when one of those eyes winked slyly. Then Beaver Brown passed along his way.

Chapter 18

Beaver on Guard

As any old-time cow puncher will admit, the backbone of a round-up is not the best roper, or the bronc peeler, or the top cowhand, or the wagon boss. You might have all these and still not have a smoothly working outfit. The backbone of the cow outfit is the cook. And the SL outfit had lost the best cook they had ever been able to hire.

Before the cowboys left Fort Shaw, over on Sun River, Till Driscoll had hired a cook. A cook who was to take the place of "Snowball," who had been recognized as a deserter from the army. Snowball was in jail at Fort Benton, and in spite of all efforts to buy him out, the military authorities told Till Driscoll that it was a matter of weeks, perhaps months until Snowball would be a free man. This news Till had broken as gently as possible to his crew of Texas cowboys who were starting back down the trail with some horses the SL had bought at Great Falls.

"We've done lost our Snowball, boys. It's hard lines, but Uncle Sammy has got him branded with his U.S. iron and won't vent the brand."

"Them biscuits he made," groaned a cowboy, a reminiscent look in his eyes, "was my idee of angel grub."

"Them pies he built," added another, "man, I could eat me a dozen!"

"And the coffee that black rascal always had hot of a wet night when a boy come in off guard! Mamma!"

"Them beans! And them steaks! And them chickens he fixed the night after we raided that hencoop down on the Muddy."

"And his son-of-a-gun-in-the-sack. With brandy sauce!"

"And the way he could pick a banjo, remember, of a starry night!"

"No way of buyin' him back off the Uncle, Till?"

"I've done my durnedest, cowhands."

Till had some more business at Fort Shaw and had sent the outfit on down the trail. He'd catch them later on. He put a cowhand called "Taller Flanks" in charge. Taller Flanks was a heavyset veteran of the trail. Likewise he was the heaviest eater in the SL outfit.

From Sun River to Fort Benton things

had gone wrong. The horses Till had bought kept trying to get back to their home range. There were rains that made the going hard. Mud. Bogged wagons. Wet tobacco. And, worst of all, a cranky cook that, according to unanimous vote, was the sorriest cook that ever rassled a Dutch oven. By the time it got to Fort Benton, the outfit was ripe for mutiny.

"The dad-burned grub spoiler ain't even clean," growled one of the cowboys. "His dish towels looks like he'd wiped the wagon wheels off. And he smells like a skinned muskrat."

They pitched camp on the bank of the Missouri near Fort Benton. The cowboys eyed the supper set out by the cook who had gained the name of "Greasy George." With town a few miles away, the SL cowhands quit complaining. They had little to say as they turned loose their horses and gathered in the mess tent. It was like a calm before the storm. Perhaps Taller Flanks smelled trouble, for he stayed with the cavvy.

A cowboy tipped over a skillet filled with soggy gravy. Now a Dutch oven filled with half-cooked beans was tipped over. The insipid coffee and greasy stew now went out on the ground. Willing hands collared the snarling, cursing cook. A rope was fastened around his waist. And they dragged him to the river's edge.

"This is the bath you been missin', Greasy."

The bank was high, the water below was deep. The cook made quite a splash as he hit the river. Sputtering, gasping, calling for help, he floundered in the water. He could not swim. Now they ducked him under, then pulled him up to let him dangle in the air. Again and again. Then they pulled him out and let him lay, gasping, sodden, spewing water, on the bank.

"Show up at camp, you grub ruiner, and we'll give you a longer bath and your carcass will be found down about St. Louis!"

They saddled up and started for town. Taller Flanks apparently had seen nothing, heard nothing. He said nothing as his cowboys started for Fort Benton. But there was a gleam of satisfaction in his eyes as he helped the day men take the remuda to where the grass grew tallest.

"Shore a nice sunset," he said to the men on herd. "Shore purty. I reckon the storms is about over."

As the SL cowboys rode, one of them was singing a song:

"Oh, I started up the trail on June
      the twenty-third,
Started up the trail with the SL herd,
Come a ti yi yippy yi yay.

"Oh, it' been bacon and beans 'most
      ever day,
And we'll soon be grazin' on
      prairie hay.

"Hired a cook for the sour-dough
      batter
The dad-burned fool couldn't even
      boil water.
Come a ti yi yippy yi yay."

Snowball leaped from his bunk. He grabbed his banjo. The next moment his resonant voice gave echo to the song of the passing cowboys. With a wild yelp they spurred their horses up to the jail wall. Tears streamed down Snowball's ebony face as they shook hands with him through the bars and told him how much they missed him and his grub and his banjo. He choked up so that he could hardly talk.

"Boss-man Till Driscoll gonna git ol' Snowball free fum dis heah jail?" he asked, his face gleaming with hope.

They exchanged wide grins.

"Just sit and say nothin', you rascal," said one of the cowboys in a low tone. "Wrap that banjo so she won't bust and be awake about second-third guard time. See you later."

They rode away before Boone could get to shake hands with them. Snowball, hanging to the bars, was laughing and weeping, his wide feet, bare of shoes or socks, shuffling in a dance step.

" 'Em mah cowboys. Dawg mah cats iffen ah don't git the wrinkles outa 'em SL hombres. Ol' Snowball gonna git 'em boys hawg fat in jes' no time. Wid a son-of-a-gun every day. Cawn bread an' biscuits. Pie an' hot coffee. Shucks, 'ey looks plumb ga'nt, fo' a fac'." He did a dance, cutting all kinds of fancy pigeon wings. Suddenly he stopped.

"Heah what 'em boys o' mine say? 'Ey is a-comin' back by de light o' de moon fo to git me. Dey bus' dis heah jail right down. Dey's yankin' mah black hide right outa heah. And dey'll be a-takin' you 'long wid 'em, sho' as you-all is alive. White man, we's about to go yondehly. Glory me, dis is sho' ouah happy day."

Boone shook his head. "I reckon I'll be a-stayin', Snowball. Runnin' off would look like I was guilty. It wouldn't be treatin' my friends right if I was to pull out. I'm gonna stick here and fight her out."

The sheriff came with their supper. He seemed to be worrying about something. While the prisoners ate, Boone could hear him up front in his office, whistling tunelessly as he paced back and forth.

There came a tap on the bars. Boone went to the window. Beaver's voice came cautiously out of the dusk.

"That you, Boone?"

"Yes, what do you want, Beaver?"

"Just lettin' ye know I done located Jawbone. I got his hidin' place located on Shonkin Creek and I'm a-watchin' him. They got ye in tight, ain't they, laddie? But they ain't a-hangin' yet, they ain't. It takes a heap of evidence to hang a man. It's ol' Beaver as knows that. It's Tex Harmer and his bunch as ye'll need worry about. They're a-ribbin' a lynchin'. Somewhere's out of town, they're a-holdin' a meetin' tonight. And mayhap they'll be a-comin' for ye, laddie. So I fetched ye this." He pushed a six-shooter and a buckskin sack full of cartridges through the bars. Before Boone could thank him, or ask more questions, the trapper was gone.

Boone quickly hid the gun and cartridges under his blankets. None too quickly, for the sheriff came after the dishes. The sheriff looked grim and worried. He said little, and soon went away.

Snowball's eyes rolled with excitement.

"Ah ain't got no fondness fer 'em lynchin's," he whispered. "You-all bettah go 'long wid me an' mah SL boys. Ain' no lynchers gonna git you 'way fum 'em boys."

Boone grinned. "Don't worry. I got somethin' now that'll kinda discourage 'em. While they're gettin' a meal, I'll get a bite or two. I'm standin' my hand." He examined the long-barrelled Colt gun to make sure it was in working order, then hid it again.

Chapter 19

Plain Talk

Uptown, the SL cowboys drank but little. They wandered around town, taking an occasional drink, no more. Bit by bit they picked up the story of Judge Lee's shooting, the escape of Jawbone, and the jailing of Boone. The talk against Boone was bitter. All sorts of crimes were hung on his name. The SL cowboys said nothing. They liked Boone and wanted to do something to help him. With that idea in mind, they hunted up the sheriff. They found him in the Gold Bug, talking to Ken Hanley.

"Us boys," said the spokesman for the SL outfit, "knows this Boone boy that you got locked up. We'd do a heap for him. If he needs money or any kind of help, we'll stand the price."

"It might be," said the sheriff grimly, "that I'll have to call on you boys later on. There's some talk about lynchin', but I dunno if they'll tackle it. Ken Hanley here is Boone's friend. We been talkin' her over.

Ken's boys are in town, and will lend a hand. But I don't want any gun battle if I can help it. Ain't you boys from the SL outfit?"

"That's our brand, sheriff."

"I got a Negro locked up that claims he cooked for the SL."

"Yeh?" A look of innocence spread across the faces of the SL cowboys. "We've had a lot of cooks. He might be one of 'em."

"He claims Till Driscoll is goin' to get him free. I hope so, for he's a good boy."

"Mebbeso he'll get free, then. Well, sheriff, when you need us, just holler. We'll be mopin' around somewheres. And we'd be just mighty proud to meet up with them parties as aim to lynch our pardner, Boone. You got a guard at the jail?"

"Couple of Ken's boys is ridin' around down there."

"That's a good idee," said an SL cow puncher. "How would it be if a couple of us rode on down to relieve 'em after a while?"

"They've been on about an hour now," said Ken Hanley. "I was goin' to send my two oldest sons down to spell 'em."

"Our boss give us warnin' he'd fire any of us that got drunk," grinned the cowboy, "and this temptation around Fort Benton is shore strong. It's a-wearin' us down, somethin' fearful. Mebbeso we better fork our ponies and take along a bottle an' ride herd on your jail."

"Suit yourselves, boys," grinned the sheriff. "If that lynchin' party saw a crowd down there on guard, it might take a lot of the notions outa their systems. But mind, boys, no shootin' by a single one of you unless you just have to shoot."

"We learned many a long day ago to keep our guns in their scabbards. Us boys is aimin' to go back to Texas. We ain't dickerin' for no golden harps, whatever."

The sheriff and Ken Hanley watched them as they rode swiftly down the street.

"You don't reckon they'll try to steal Boone outa jail, Ken?"

"Dunno. They might try. But somehow I'd lay a big bet that the boy wouldn't run. He's no quitter, and he's got good reason for wantin' to clear himself. For unless I'm gettin' blind, Boone and that baby girl of Judge Lee's is kinda fond of one another. Just kid fancy, but it'll do a lot for a boy like Boone. It's what he needs. When Bill said in his letter that the boy was a high-strung colt, he hit the nail on the head. Well, I'm goin' over to the hospital to see

160

how the judge is comin' on. Doc says he has an even chance unless somethin' sets in to poison his blood. Got any line on the Jawbone gent?"

"Not yet, Ken. I've got three-four posses out. That's what has throwed me short-handed here in case of a jail delivery. Lucky them SL boys come to town."

"Virginia says that this Jawbone stepped up to the judge and said somethin' to him that she didn't ketch. The judge stepped back like he was startled, and his hand went to his chest. He's had a couple of heart attacks the past few years, and mebbeso one took him. This Jawbone, drunk and on the kill, thought the judge was goin' for his gun, I reckon. So he cut loose. When the judge gets conscious and can talk, he might be able to clear up this business. That is, if he'll talk."

"What do you mean, Ken?"

"It just might be that there's some things in his past life that Judge Lee wouldn't want to talk about. Things he's buried deep."

"Most of us," said the sheriff, "can look back and remember things we done that was wrong. The man that never was wrong, Ken, wouldn't be fit to judge the faults of others. I've wondered a lot about that, and I knowed that Judge Lee must have made his mistakes because he is so fair on the bench. Well, see you later, Ken."

The sheriff prowled the streets, listening, watching, keeping the pulse of his town. He looked for Jeremy Lee, but the river gambler was nowhere to be found. Lieutenant Clanton, he knew, was at the hospital. But Jeremy Lee and Tex Harmer were not to be found. They had been seen together once or twice, so the sheriff drew his own conclusions.

Now a man on horseback came down the street. The sheriff hailed him. The rider was one of his deputies.

"Locate 'em?"

"They're gathered about five miles down the river. Harmer's the big chief. No sign of the gambler, though. They plan to break into the jail at midnight. They'll try to rush it, I reckon. There must be a hundred men in the mob."

"There's about fifteen SL cowhands down at the jail now. There's ten of Ken Hanley's boys scattered around town. And there must be some more men in Fort Benton that stand for law and order strong enough to side against these drunken hoodlums. And when the sign shows danger, I'm givin' Boone a gun and lettin' him use it. The man I want to see now is this Jeremy Lee, the judge's nephew."

"He's a slick un, sheriff."

"Slick? I'll tell a man! And dangerous."

The sheriff would have been doubly convinced could he have been witness to a little scene being enacted in a cabin down on the river bank.

Jeremy Lee and a roughly garbed man faced one another across a table on which stood a lighted candle. The two tied holsters on the other man's thighs were empty of weapon. Jeremy Lee, his handsome face inscrutable, his black eyes glittering from under the straight black brows, took his own guns and extracted the loads. Then he walked to the door and, opening it, dropped the guns outside. Now he locked the door and put the key in his waistcoat pocket. The bearded, roughly clad man, eyed him with venomous glance, his coarse lips sneering.

Now the river gambler removed his coat, and from an inside pocket took a package wrapped in brown paper. His slender, well-kept hands undid the package. From the paper he took two brand new bowie knives. With a deft twist of his wrist, he stuck one of the knives in the table within an inch of where one of the burly fellow's hands rested. The man jerked back his hand, the sneer gone from his lips. Jeremy Lee smiled as he balanced the other knife in his hand.

"Now, brother Fouchet, you and I will play a little two-handed game. I tricked you into coming here so that, before I killed you, we would meet, just the two of us, alone, and face to face. Your clumsy shooting ruined a good hat for me. Twice before you've tried to kill me. But luck favored me. You followed me here from St. Louis. I thought I recognized you among the crowd on the boat, but I couldn't be positive. Then I saw you in a saloon here, talking business with the Jawbone party. Shortly after which you tried to shoot me, and almost succeeded. Fouchet, one of us will leave this cabin alive. In a moment I'll put out the light. We'll be in the dark, each with a knife. I could have shot you when I had the drop, and made you throw away your guns. I could have killed you a moment ago when I flipped that knife into the table instead of into your heart. Notice that the point is buried a good two inches in the wood. It's a trick I learned from a knife thrower in Mexico.

"But I didn't kill you, Fouchet. I want

you in the dark, with the fear of death chilling your black heart. I hate to see a man die. But in the dark, Fouchet, I won't be able to see you. I'll only hear the death rattle in your throat as you lie there on the floor. Giving you a knife is, to be frank with you, just a matter of form. Because the instant that candlelight goes out, the knife in my hand will slide through the darkness before you can move, and this six-inch blade will be buried to the hilt in your heart. I am waiting, brother Fouchet, for you to pick up your knife."

The man backed away from the weapon, fear widening his eyes.

"It'll be murder. I'm no knife man. I'll fight you any other way, but not with a knife. A knife is a greaser weapon. I — I always had a fear of knife cuts."

"Most men have," smiled the river gambler. "That is why I chose these nice bowie knives. I love the feel of a well-balanced knife. I spent two hours finding the ones I wanted." Jeremy Lee leaned across the table.

"I am about to blow out the light, Fouchet."

"Don't! Gosh, man, don't! Don't kill me like that! Take a gun and shoot me! But not that way, Lee! Not a knife."

Slobbering, his lips trembling, the burly coward dropped to his knees, his hands gripping the table edge, begging and whimpering for his life.

"Gimme a chance! Say, gimme a chance! I can tell you somethin' that'll keep you from bein' killed! There's others beside me want to see you dead. I'll tell you everything. And I'll pull out and go away where you'll never see me no more! I'll swear it! Gimme a chance to talk, Jeremy Lee!"

Not a muscle of the river gambler's countenance changed. His voice was cold, deadly, without mercy, when he spoke.

"Talk then, Fouchet. Talk fast. And talk straight. If you lie, I'll know it and this knife will slide into your black heart. Commence!"

Fear kept the cringing man to the truth. For half an hour he talked in halting, broken, whispered sentences, while the candlelight guttered, throwing weird shadows across the crude walls.

Jeremy Lee, his face mask-like, save for a merciless smile, listened to every word. He had slipped into his coat, and when Fouchet had done speaking, he unlocked the door. As he stepped outside, the burly man followed. As the river gambler picked up his two empty guns, a gun roared in the renegade's hand. But Jeremy Lee had leaped to one side. The tiny derringer that had somehow filled the gambler's hand barked twice. Fouchet, with a snarling, gasping moan, slid to the floor. His heavy body twitched convulsively, then lay without a movement.

Jeremy Lee stood over him, reloading the dangerous little derringer that had taken the other man's life.

"I figured you'd try it, Fouchet," he said coldly to the dead man; "that's why I left your gun where you'd make a break for it. You understand, Fouchet, that you knew too much. You simply had to die. It was in the cards from the beginning."

He closed the door on the dead man and walked back to town. He did not slacken his brisk pace until he reached the hospital.

"Has Judge Lee regained consciousness?" he asked of the surgeon.

"He has. But his condition is precarious. There is something that troubles his mind. Without that mental burden, he'd have a fair chance for recovery."

Jeremy Lee nodded. "Tell him that I called, doctor. And give him this message from me. Tell him that Raoul Fouchet is dead. The judge will understand. And the message will lift a part of the burden that weighs on his mind and heart."

As Jeremy Lee was leaving, he met Lieutenant Harry Clanton in the hallway. The young army officer seemed to be in a bad humor. The river gambler's eyebrow lifted questioningly.

"She won't give me any satisfaction about that horse," the officer growled. "And she handed out some rather nasty remarks. You're her cousin, why don't you try to get it out of her where the horse is?"

"I'm an attorney, old chap, not a detective. Besides, my fair cousin's opinion of me is not the highest, to put it mildly. As I recall her words, she described me as a card sharper, a black sheep, and a trickster. But she's your fiancée, I believe."

"She was," corrected Lieutenant Clanton with a frigid smile. "She broke the engagement a few minutes ago. She's championing that horse thief. I've a mind to chuck the whole thing."

"That," shrugged Jeremy Lee, "is wholly up to you, lieutenant. I'm merely your attorney in the matter of this horse-stealing case. And unless you produce the horse, we have absolutely no case against the Boone fellow. There are thousands of bay horses. It's up to us to prove ownership of the horse that he rode into town, then sent out to the judge's ranch. You must understand, old fellow, that I'll have other things to attend to, and cannot be using valuable time hunting this horse. As you know, Boone can and probably will demand immediate trial. And if we have no horse to show the twelve good men and true, where is our case against him?"

"I'll get the horse, with or without your help. Confound it, I'm doing all the work on this case!"

Jeremy Lee selected a long, black cheroot from a seal-skin case and painstakingly lit it. His hands were steady. Lieutenant Clanton did not notice the tiny trickle of blood that came down the coat sleeve of the river gambler. Fouchet's bullet had torn through his coat and shirt, grazing the skin just enough to draw blood.

"My dear Clanton," smiled Jeremy Lee, "I must repeat that I am merely an attorney at law, not a detective. When I am not engaged in the legal profession, I gain a certain relaxation from the gaming tables. As your legal adviser, I would suggest that you utilize your spare moments in getting absolute possession of this bay gelding."

"And as a friend, what would you advise in regard to Virginia?"

"Friend?" Jeremy Lee smiled thinly. "Since when have we been friends? I have no friend. True, we went to military school together. Old family ties and all that. But since you went to West Point, and I chose Mexico as a university of higher education, our paths have gone apart. I am, as my fair cousin so aptly puts it, a trickster, a black-leg, and more or less of a villain. I trust no man. Few men put faith in me. My advice is worthless because I seldom give it without having a selfish motive. I am fettered by no silly codes. I live by my wits, my ability as a gambler at any man's game, and this little toy." He held in the palm of his hand the little derringer pistol.

Lieutenant Clanton stepped back a pace under the glitter of the river gambler's eye. Jeremy Lee laughed softly.

"I've always wondered why you chose an army career, Harry. You hate guns. You're afraid of this little pistol. Your father was a minister. I can still recall his insipid sermons. Insipid, because the preacher had never done wrong, had never erred, had hidden always behind a barrier of one sort or another. Even as you've been sheltered, from the days when you crept behind your nurse to throw rocks at the poor children in the streets.

"You chose the army as a stepping-stone to wealth. You've had easy tasks because you used influence. You've gone up in rank above better men than you are. You've bought your way, always. And the men who took your money know what you are. A word from me would put you out of the United States Army, Clanton. Because the army is a man's game, and you aren't a man. It takes more than an act of Congress to make a man an officer and a gentleman. It takes grit to be a cavalry officer. You've never seen a battle. You've never had a gun shoved into your stomach. You've done paper work at a desk, protected by the shavetails and the yellow-striped gents in blue uniforms that think the United States cavalry is Uncle Sam's toughest branch of the service. Which it is. And those same meat-eating cavalry soldiers have tasted dust, and snow, and hail, and rain, and thirst, on campaigns that you never saw. And with them went officers who died with a sabre in one hand and a Colt gun in the other.

"It's men like you, Clanton, that make the civilian hate a soldier. And it is men like Crook and Custer that make the Western men take off their hats when they remember their names. You want advice?

171

Then get it! Get it from a man that's a river gambler, an outcast, a blackleg. A man who claims no one of the virtues. Get out of the army before you're kicked out. You don't belong there, Clanton, any more than I belong in the society of decent men and women. You're a limber-spined quitter. If you were not, you'd knock me down. This little pistol just killed a man. And, Clanton, it may kill you. You ask my advice regarding Virginia Lee. Well, you'll get it. Stay away from my cousin. I reckon you can understand what I mean."

Jeremy Lee's voice had never gone above that cold, impersonal tone that could not be heard fifteen feet away. He was smiling, and his black eyes were as opaque as ever. Lieutenant Clanton's face was drained of color. His pale eyes showed fear. The river gambler smiled crookedly.

"You must be drunk, Jeremy, or crazy," gasped the army officer.

"I think not, Clanton. I'm sober. I hope I'm sane. You rather forced the issue."

"You're a common gambler. A disgrace to your family name. I'll take no orders from you in my personal affairs." Harry Clanton's fists clenched. His white face was twisted with fury.

"That's the first time," said Jeremy Lee

coldly, "that I ever saw you show fight. Nurse it along. Then hunt me up. Coffee and pistols for two, old fellow. Any time. Any place. And I hope I won't have to throw any further insults your way to force the duel. Good day, you —"

And Jeremy Lee, having flung the fighting name in the other man's face, strode by him and out of the door. He tossed away his cheroot and lit a fresh one. Then he sauntered up the street to the sheriff's office.

Chapter 20

Snake Tracks

Some one was singing softly: "Oh, I started up the trail on June the third —"

"Dey's come for ol' Snowball," grinned the black-faced prisoner in the Fort Benton jail.

"Got your banjo wrapped up?" asked Boone.

"In a blanket, wrapped tight."

Ropes were tossed in. Snowball and Boone made them fast to the window bars.

"All set, you son of a black kittle?"

Snowball grinned happily at the familiar tone, and flung back:

"Hahd and fast. Cowhands, do yoh best!"

A dozen ropes snagged to five iron bars. Stout horses and stout saddle-trees. Wild cowboys and a sickle moon. Some ropes snapped, some held. Iron bent under the stout pressure, pulling loose from the cottonwood logs. Out yonder in the dark a rope got under a horse's tail, and the popping of stirrups told the story of a cowboy who had grabbed for a saddle horn and picked a handful of dirt.

"Three bars off, Snowball. Climb through, you biscuit builder! Are you there, Boone?"

"Here and nowhere else, cowboys." He boosted Snowball through the window and stood there, looking out at the cowboys who grouped around there.

"Rattle your hocks, Boone. We ain't got much time to waste. Somebody's comin'."

"Sorry boys, but I can't go along. I have to stick here."

"They're aimin' to hang you, pardner."

"Well, I won't be the first man that ever stretched rope. I got some friends kinda dependin' on me to come clear at this trial. If I was to cut and run, it wouldn't be fair to them, savvy?"

The quiet finality of Boone's voice checked any further argument.

Snowball bade Boone a husky so-long, then was taken away on horseback. Now a large group of horsemen came slowly toward the jail.

"I reckon," said an SL cowboy, "that here comes our meat. Got a shootin' iron, Boone?"

"Yep. You boys better clear out. I don't

want anybody to get shot on my account. I reckon I can make out all right."

"Yeah? What kind of an outfit do you think us SL boys is, Boone? We ain't runnin' from Tex Harmer's skunks."

Now, between the jail and the oncoming riders, rode three men. The sheriff, Ken Hanley, and Jeremy Lee.

Boone climbed out of the window, vaulting into the empty saddle of the horse they had brought him. There was a Winchester in the saddle scabbard.

"I reckon I'll go along, boys," he told them. "I'll see you later. One of you men tell the sheriff I made a get-away."

With a wild yell, Boone jumped his horse into a run. He headed for the river.

"Ketch me if you can, Harmer!" he yelled, and rode away in a hail of bullets.

"Looks like the joke is on us," said the sheriff. He pointed to the racing Boone and the angry mob that was in hot pursuit.

"Nothing we can do now," said Ken Hanley. "Doggone me if I believed that boy would rabbit on us!"

Now the SL men came up. They grinned boldly at the sheriff.

"Boone chawed them bars apart, sheriff, and got clean away. He's forkin' a horse that can outrun anything around here. One of the horses Till Driscoll bought. Now, ain't it just a dad-burned shame about his runnin' off from a nice, comfortable jail that a way? How do yuh reckon he got out, sheriff?"

"That," said the sheriff, "is somethin' that will probably always remain a mystery." The sheriff's tone was an edge sharp. "Boone shore fooled me. I figgered he was man enough to stay and take his medicine."

"Hold on, sheriff," said one of the SL cow punchers. "I wouldn't go sayin' that Boone was a coward. The way I size up the situation is like this: that Boone didn't want nobody hurt on his account. So he runs for it, and that mob of lynchers a-trailin' him, pourin' bullets at him. He'll lose 'em in the dark. He'll bust that ol' river open wherever he comes to the bank. And I'm layin' odds that not many of them brave and fearless lynchin' gents will foller him into the water. You'll see some more of that cowhand. If he's a coward, then I wish I was one just like him."

"Well spoken," said Jeremy Lee in a flat-toned voice. He lit a cheroot, and the flare of the match showed, for a brief moment, his thin-lipped smile.

"Who might you be?" asked the cow-puncher.

"I might be almost any one, friend. I have been called many names, none of which carried a compliment. I spoke because I was impressed by your loyalty to another man. Loyalty is a virtue I don't possess, but admire in others." The river gambler turned to the sheriff and Ken Hanley.

"Unless you need me, I'll be getting along my way."

The sheriff scowled. "You're a hard cuss to figger out. Judge Lee is a fine man, and you're his nephew, but I'd be lyin' if I said I'd trust you. Whatever your game is, you shore keep your cards close."

"If I didn't, sheriff," said Jeremy Lee, "I'd have been planted in some boot hill long ago. Am I under arrest?"

"I'm sorry," said the sheriff, "but you're not. It looks to me like you're playin' both ends against the middle. You get the Boone gent arrested. Then you side in against your friends that's aimin' to lynch him. Wherever you go, there's snake tracks."

"When a man lives by his wits, sheriff, he must protect himself. I claim no allegiance to any man. I owe no man any debt of gratitude. No man owes me, sheriff, anything but a debt of hatred. Gentlemen,

I bid you good night."

Jeremy Lee rode away alone into the night. He was whistling softly as he sat his horse. He came to the river bank and spurred his reluctant mount into the black stream. As horse and man hit swimming water, the river gambler held his gun and cartridge belt above his head so as to keep them dry.

Chapter 21

Why? Why?

When he left the jail, Boone rode hard for the river. The horse between his legs was strong and fast. Between mount and rider was that bond of understanding that only a horseman can know when he feels the strength of bone and muscle and a staunch heart in the horse under him.

Bullets sprayed the night's blackness. Ahead was a high bank. Below, the river muttered and whirled in its channel. Boone lifted his weight in the stirrups. His head lay along the sleek neck.

"Take it, boy, take the water!"

A splash. The crack of guns behind. Boone came to the water's surface, clinging to the tail of the swimming horse. The water was black as a cavern. Bullets cut the swirling river. The quick plunge into the cold water sent the boy's blood pounding. On the high bank behind him he could hear the shouts and profane orders that were not obeyed by the men who dared not tackle the treacherous river in the darkness.

Now a man spurred into the water. But no man followed Tex Harmer as he pushed his horse into the swift current. Alone, the killer of the Harmer clan followed Boone across the black river.

An undercurrent swept Boone and his horse into a whirlpool. For minutes man and horse fought the treacherous current. A big cottonwood snag entangled them, and Boone, risking death from the threshing, shod hoofs, swam around the horse and cleared the terrified animal.

Behind him, somewhere on that inky water, Boone could hear the loud breathing of a swimming horse. And the muttered cursing of its rider. Boone reached for his gun. It was gone. The weapon had slid out of its holster. But there was still the Winchester carbine in the saddle scabbard. Boone swam alongside the horse and hung to the saddle horn. The strong current pulled them downstream. Now they were nearing the opposite shore. With a sudden sinking of hope, Boone saw that they were facing a sheer clay bank. It needed every bit of his horse savvy and his cool courage to save himself and the horse from drowning. He slapped his hat against the gelding's head, so as to start the horse downstream. To touch bridle rein now would mean disaster, for few horses can be reined in the water. They will fall backward. Boone now loosened the latigo strap so as to ease off the cinch pressure.

The swimming horse, game of heart in spite of terror, struck out with the current. Boone hung to the long tail. Down, down along that sheer bank, where the clay bluff rose fifty feet against the star-filled sky. The gurgling, muttering current tugged with insidious, slimy clutch at man and horse. Now a whirlpool sucked them below the surface. The horse, ears filled with water, fought with insane fright. Boone, swimming ahead, felt the dangerous nearness of the forefeet of the horse that floundered with terrified desperation. Now a shod hoof grazed Boone's cheek. The fear-maddened animal was on top of him.

Boone dived under. His lungs seemed to be bursting. Blackness, black as only black water can be, enveloped him. His brain spun like a top. Then that terrified struggle of one who is drowning. That smothering sensation. The river whirling him like a submerged bit of driftwood. Then a freak current pulled him to the surface. His lungs filled with air. Water spilled from his mouth and nose. He floundered about. The horse was climbing ashore on a slippery bank. Boone grabbed at some willows and pulled himself up on to a sand bar. There he lay, gasping, half-drowned, spouting water.

Now, out there in the black river, a riderless horse swam with empty saddle, fighting the swift currents. The horse snorted and puffed. On downstream. Boone, only half-conscious, wondered what had become of the rider. He reckoned it was Tex Harmer who had dared tackle the black river in pursuit. And, half-drowned, his head dizzy, his lungs aching, Boone wondered why Harmer so hated him. He had never harmed the Texan. Yet the man seemed more intent on seeing Boone killed than he was bent on killing Jawbone Smith. There must be some strong motive to cause such a desire to kill. The half-drowned boy lay there on the sand bar that was covered with a willow thicket, trying to think. Well, anyhow, he had prevented a bitter fight back at the jail.

Now a cottonwood log, half-submerged, floated downstream. And to it clung a man. Boone, peering through the willows, could make out the blob of his head and shoulders. He could hear the laboured breathing of the man as he fought to steer the log shoreward. Man and log slid past in the night. Boone reckoned he would land below on the long, sandy bar. Time to be moving along.

Boone scrambled up the bank and caught his horse that stood, reins dropped, up on the bank above the water. He tightened the saddle cinch, slid the Winchester from its boot, and rode away. His direction led south along Shonkin Creek, and he rode warily. He figured that probably the rest of Harmer's posse had got across by now at the easier crossing. The night might hold a score of men eager to shoot him out of the saddle. The heavy-calibered gun weighted his arm, and he laid it across the saddle in front of him as he took in the surrounding country with keen eyes.

This country was familiar to Boone, as he had come to Fort Benton by way of the Shonkin. There was a cow outfit or two that ranged their stuff in here. And he recalled a deserted cabin that was well hidden in the hills at the edge of the Highwoods. He could hide there until the hunt for him died out. Then he would start out to find Jawbone, and when he found him, he would make the renegade talk even if he had to torture the truth from him. Boone had made up his mind to get to the truth of his heritage and learn the mystery that had clouded his boyhood. Beaver Brown had said Jawbone was hiding on Shonkin Creek. He'd be mighty well hidden, too. Jawbone was slick about finding a place to hole up. Beaver had tracked him to his hiding place and was watching him. Why? There was another queer kink in it! What did Beaver want of Jawbone? Did he aim to kill him? It didn't look that a way, or he'd have done it before this and fetched in Jawbone for the reward on him, dead or alive. Beaver had some other notion in his shaggy head. Beaver was slick as a fox. A man couldn't trust him too far. Still, he'd slipped Boone that gun there at the jail. Boone reckoned the trapper was a little cracked in the brain. A lot of those old trail blazers did queer things. They led queer lives, living alone, for the most part, or with Indians, facing all kinds of dangers, suffering all manner of bitter hardships that would kill ordinary men.

Boone saw a camp fire, but avoided it. He daren't take a chance on riding into strange camps. So he gave the fire a wide berth and kept on. He thought he saw the fire suddenly go out, and it struck him as being odd. He had gone some distance when he caught the sound of a distant rifle shot. He pulled up, listening. But there came no repetition of the shot. Better be movin' along. Let well enough alone, he thought.

And so Boone missed running into Beaver Brown and Jawbone Smith. For it was Jawbone's fire that had suddenly gone out. And it was Jawbone's long-barrelled rifle that had cracked the night's silence.

Chapter 22

In the Night

Now, Jawbone Smith was not much of a hand at taking stock in ghosts. But since he had gone crazy drunk and shot Judge Lee, then almost drowned making his get-away across the river, he'd heard things in his sleep that made him wonder if a ghost was a-follerin' him. There was a bullet hole in Jawbone's shoulder that, while it wasn't no ways serious, kept him from sleepin' good. He was afoot, too, and that bothered him, because he always liked a horse near in case he needed to run for it. But there wasn't much danger of ever bein' found here at this old cave in the rim rocks. He'd had foresight, he told himself, to lay in a grub supply and plenty whisky here at the cave. And no man except himself knew its location. Some day before long some cowboy would be riding that way after cattle, and he'd drop him out of his saddle with a bullet between his shoulders. He had plenty of cartridges for the rifle that he'd planted there with the grub and the whisky. Even if he didn't have a horse, he was safer here than ridin' the hills, skylightin' hisself.

But at night, them danged noises kep' him sittin' in the dark, cold shivers chillin' him. And no matter how drunk he got, the noises kep' botherin'. He laid it to the noise of the crick and the wind in the tree-tops. And daytimes, when he looked around, he couldn't find any sign.

"I must be a-gettin' the jimjams again," he muttered, and built himself a fire to chase away the blackness. He took frequent pulls at his jug, and never let go his rifle. He stared out past the firelight rim until his eyeballs ached. Sometimes, when he couldn't stand it no longer, he'd curse in a croaking voice, challenging that unseen thing that chuckled and muttered just like Beaver Brown used to. And Beaver was dead. Jawbone had killed Beaver, down in New Mexico. He'd shot him and left him for the buzzards, after he'd robbed the dead man's pockets. Now the old son wouldn't stay dead! He'd commenced comin' back of a night to spoil Jawbone's sleep and peace of mind with his eternal chuckling and muttering.

Odd, too, how Beaver's scent was there when the breeze was right. Beaver's clothes always was saturated with animal odors. Kind of a mixture of skunk and muskrat. Sickish sort of smell. It was that smell, and the man's ever-lastin' chucklin' and mutterin' that drove Jawbone to kill him, as much as it was the gold Beaver kep' in the buckskin sack hung around his middle.

All day long Jawbone's shoulder and his other old wounds had ached fit to drive a man loco. That meant a storm a-comin'. He limped around, stupid with drink, crippled with pains and aches, cursing, and whimpering and snarling, like some tortured beast. Come dark, he'd ketched that scent in the wind. Muskrat and skunk smell. He took his gun and prowled around over the rocks and through the brush patches. And finally he built a fire, risking the danger of its light being seen. He pulled the corn cob from his jug's mouth and drank heavily. Fear showed in his shifting eyes, and its stamp could be seen on his whisky-blurred face. He had drunk a lot that day. More than his usual amount. He was trying to deaden the pain of his bullet-scarred body, trying to drug his brain until he could crawl up in his rim-rock cave and sleep.

Now, instead of his brain getting numb,

it began playing scurvy tricks on him. He could hear Beaver's annoying chuckling and muttering. The odor of musk and skunk hung in the air, filling Jawbone's nostrils, seeping into his brain until he felt smothered. With a sudden fear of the fire-light, he took a short-handled shovel and threw dirt on the fire, snarling and whining like a wolf the while. He blotted out the last bit of fire. Now he'd lost the location of his jug, and crawled around on all fours hunting it. Beaver's chuckling seemed close behind him. He staggered to his feet. Something moved, there in that brush. With a thin scream, Jawbone shot at the shadow. He ran toward it, stumbled, fell. Now a heavy weight dropped on him. Hands like steel bands held him close against the ground. His rifle was jerked out of his hands and flung aside. Beaver's chuckling filled his brain. That heavy odor was stifling him, shutting off his wind, smothering him. Something seemed to snap in Jawbone's whisky-warped brain, and he lay there, sobbing, whimpering, his face hidden in the dirt, begging some one, any one, to take away this dead man that was haunting him till he'd gone mad.

Stout deer-hide thongs bound the ankles of Jawbone. Then rough hands jerked him to a sitting position.

"I been waitin' a long time," cackled Beaver, "to spend a nice evenin' with my ol' pard with meat in my mouth and whisky in the jug. Just me an' ol' Jawbone, him as et my grub, and used my blankets, and got full on my likker. Just me and you, pard."

"Yo're dead!" muttered Jawbone, staring with burning eyes into the darkness. "Yo're dead, I say! I'm just a-dreamin' this. It's the jimmies taken a-holt of me. You ain't there. Beaver Brown is dead!"

"I'm just back for a nice, friendly visit. It gets almighty lonesome for me where I live. So, thinks I, I'll hunt up my ol' pard, Jawbone, and nibble at his jug and smoke his terbaccer."

"You lie, you lie!" croaked Jawbone.

A chuckling muttering came from the darkness. The gurgle of the jug. Jawbone Smith begged for a drink of whisky, but the chuckling and muttering of Beaver Brown mocked him into a whining, snarling rage. Jawbone's shaking fingers fought at the buckskin thongs, but without success. The tiny knot of buckskin, wet before it was tied, would require patience, steady hands, and daylight to unravel. Nor could Jawbone break the twisted bit of wet hide. As

191

well try to break wire.

"Set there, pard," chuckled Beaver, "Set there while ol' Beaver's ghost drinks hearty. Think of the bullet hole you put in pore ol' Beaver as had been your pardner in camp and on the trail. Ol' Beaver, the same as nursed you through fevers and the snakes. Shared his blankets, and his terbaccer, and his grub, and his jug. Then you shot him in the back one night, and robbed his poke. You'll die soon, Jawbone, and burn after. You'll go with the horrors of a hangman's noose. Or mayhap a knife shoved in your carcass, where you'll die hard and slow, and no water or whisky or a friend to mourn your passin'. And the coyotes will pick your bones. As you sow, you'll reap, Jawbone, and you've sowed naught but bad seed."

The whisky set Beaver's tongue to wagging. He babbled on, between drinks, of the old trails and the old camps. He spoke of men long dead, of murdered men who waited to meet Jawbone in the hereafter. Until the listening renegade was groveling in the dirt, not knowing if he listened to man or ghost or the mocking voice of delirium.

Now Jawbone's groping hands gripped the jug. He lifted it with a croaking cry, only to throw it aside with a curse. For the jug Beaver had set where his former pardner would find it was empty.

The empty jug found in the dark but increased the man's bewilderment, and he raved in maudlin fashion.

Apparently, Beaver had had former experiences with Jawbone, when the latter was half-crazy from whisky. For he played on the tortured man's feelings as some skilled mechanic might tinker with a bit of machinery. Now and then he put an adroit question. Jawbone would give him reply without knowing he spoke.

For an indefinite time this continued. Now and then Beaver would give the other man a slug of raw whisky. Enough to keep him conscious, afraid, and willing to answer the questions with a truth born of stark terror.

Into the questions and answers were woven the names of men. Judge Lee, Frank Boone, the man whom the judge had killed in a duel. The Harmers. The boy Boone whom Jawbone had raised. A man named Raoul Fouchet.

Until finally Jawbone, with a dull groan, dropped into a stupor.

Beaver Brown took his knife and cut the buckskin thongs. He knelt beside the unconscious Jawbone for some time, the long-bladed knife in his hand, its point touching the pit of Jawbone's stomach. Beaver's shaggy face twitched with emotion. His eyes, bright, fox-like, cunning, twinkled and glittered. Finally he rose and slid the unstained hunting knife back into its scabbard. He took a final pull at the whisky jug he had kept for himself, and set it down again.

"In the mornin'," he chuckled, looking down at the man who tossed and whimpered and groaned in his whisky-drugged sleep, "you'll wonder was it a dream or not. And the worry will ripen you for what's comin'. Better for you, Jawbone, if I slid this knife into your heart. Because it'd be more merciful, in the end."

Chuckling and muttering, Beaver slipped away into the night.

Chapter 23

Beaver Rides Sign

For Boone, hiding in the hills at the foot of the Highwoods, these next few weeks dragged past with an interminable slowness. And each day, when men rode the ridges on their man hunt, the danger of being discovered and drawn into a gun battle was simply a matter of luck. Because some chance rider, might, at any time, come spurring into the brush-filled canyon where the boy was hiding.

Boone wondered a little at the intensity of this man hunt that went on around him. He did not credit himself with such importance that a score of men or more should stay on the hunt so long. He did not guess the truth. That it was Jawbone Smith, not him, that the men were hunting, and that the sheriff of Fort Benton was leading the posse.

There had been a cold-blooded murder there on the Shonkin range. A cowboy had been shot through the back, and his horse stolen by the murderer. Because Jawbone was known to be afoot when he fled from the shooting of Judge Lee, it was but natural to suppose that he had done this second crime. And it was for Jawbone, not Boone, that the posse searched.

Now the truth of Tex Harmer's past was known at Fort Benton, Virginia Lee had recognized the man as one of the road agents, that same evening when Harmer had led his mob to attack the jail. She had met him on the street just before dark, and had remembered his face with its pocked skin when his mask had slipped off. And Harmer knew that the girl had recognized him. He had smiled twistedly and lifted his hat, then moved on.

The day following Boone's escape, Harmer's dead horse was found hung up in a big river snag. Since no man had seen Harmer since he pushed his horse into the black stream after Boone, it was natural to suppose the man was dead. If any one knew otherwise, he kept the information to himself.

Also, another man had dropped from sight. That man was Jeremy Lee, river gambler and nephew of Judge Lee, who was slowly recovering from his bullet injury. Jeremy Lee had ridden away that night of the jail-break when the sheriff lost two prisoners and the SL outfit recovered their precious cook. The river gambler vanished.

The sheriff, to the complete satisfaction of the SL outfit, was too busy with the hunt for Jawbone to be concerned over the loss of the Negro cook. The sheriff suggested that they might be doing him a favour by moving on homeward with their horses. They lost no time in taking the hint. And when Till Driscoll and Jawn R., who were starting down the trail, heard of the jail-break that had freed Snowball and Boone, the two trail bosses grinned at one another understandingly. Both men nodded when Ken Hanley 'lowed that cooks these days was scarce articles, and that where a cook was involved, almost any kind of crime to hold him had ought to be overlooked.

"But it's the Boone cowboy that kinda throwed us into feelin' like we was pore judges of humankind. We reckoned he'd stand his hand."

"And when he didn't," said Till Driscoll, "you can be shore certain the boy had his reasons. And they was strong reasons."

Ken Hanley nodded. "I look for Boone to show up one of these days."

"When he does," said Till Driscoll, "hand him this letter. It has some important information in it concernin' who was his daddy."

"How did you come by the information?" asked Ken Hanley.

"I come acrost a little notebook and some letters that Jawbone must 'a' lost. It tells the tale."

Ken Hanley took the bulky letter. His eyes met those of the trail boss, then turned to the sheriff.

"Here is what we need to cinch our own guess, I reckon. The boy is Frank Boone's son. Driscoll, you and me and Jawn R. and the sheriff had better talk this over. You know what all this will mean for Judge Lee?"

"I do," said Till Driscoll bluntly. "It'll ruin him in politics."

"After all these years, if this thing comes up again," said Ken Hanley, "it'll kill him. I'll hand this letter over to the sheriff and he'll put it in his safe. Will you trust us to do right by the boy?"

"If I didn't trust you," said Driscoll, smiling, "I wouldn't be handin' you the letter for Boone. I've got to be gettin' on back down the long trail, and can't 'tend to it myself. But while both you men are

Judge Lee's friends, I reckon you will do right by this boy who has been wronged."

"We'll see that right is right, Driscoll."

"That's all I'm askin'."

"In case the boy gets killed," said Ken Hanley, "what then?"

"Burn what's in that envelope," said the SL trail boss. "What folks don't know, won't never hurt 'em. I've never told any man what is in this envelope."

Ken Hanley nodded. "Young Boone, if he don't get shot, will come into what belongs to him."

He made no mention of the fact that Judge Lee had, when he first regained consciousness, asked for the sheriff and his old friend, Ken Hanley. The judge's face was gray with pain, and his handsome, tolerant, kindly eyes were dark with another pain that struck deeper than any bullet could penetrate.

"Find that young man named Boone. And find Jawbone Smith. A great wrong has been done and must be righted, regardless of what it may cost. Where is Jeremy, my nephew?"

"He's disappeared, judge."

"If you can find him, fetch him to me. In case I should die, there is a package in my safe marked, 'Papers concerning Frank

Boone.' They will tell you the story of a tragedy. May God forgive me for the part I have played in that tragedy!"

But the judge was recovering. And no trace had been found of Boone, Jawbone, Tex Harmer, or Jeremy Lee. Though a shaggy-haired, shaggy-bearded man in greasy buckskin, whose fox-like eyes missed nothing of what was going on, might have told of seeing, at different times, each of those four men.

The wily Beaver had witnessed the murder of the cowboy. And he had fingered the trigger of his long rifle when the murderer mounted the horse for the possession of which he had done murder. But he let the murderer go.

"Ride on, Tex Harmer. You'll hang, in the end, for this and other black crimes that your crooked mind has set your hands to do. Ride keerful, Harmer. Ride keerful, you black-hearted skunk!"

It amused Beaver to know that Jawbone was being hunted for a crime committed by Tex Harmer. The trapper gained some sort of grisly satisfaction from the error that prompted this fresh man hunt on the Shonkin.

"Be a joke on Jawbone if he was to get killed for Harmer's job."

Beaver, taking care to conceal his own movements, followed Tex Harmer to the killer's first night's camp. Then, while Harmer slept, the moccasined trapper cut the rawhide hobble and set free the killer's stolen horse.

"You'll be afoot for a spell, you pock-marked son of Satan. Aye, and there'll be the chill of fear in your heart when you come on them cut hobbles. For you'll know that whoever set you afoot has let you live a-purpose. And you'll wonder when a bullet will ketch you in the back."

Beaver had visited Jawbone later that night. Working his way on foot along the Shonkin, driven by terror from his rim-rock cave, the half-crazy Jawbone was making his way slowly out of that part of the country. And as he travelled, Beaver followed him in the dark. Chuckling and muttering, driving the brain-tortured Jaw-bone on and on through the nights.

Beaver knew where Boone was camped. Even as he knew that Jeremy Lee now rode at the head of a small band of desperate men, the former followers of Tex Harmer. What or whom that little band of hard-riding outlaws sought, Beaver could only half-surmise. It but confirmed the trap-per's suspicion that the river gambler was a road agent and a killer. The blackleg scion of a proud family. The handsome gambler was bold, clever, with a pair of quick guns, and a trained brain. Far more dangerous than any of the lesser outlaws, Jeremy Lee. He was a seasoned gambler playing for high stakes.

"When Jeremy Lee meets Boone, and if the breaks are even," chuckled the trapper, "there will be a fight worth the seein'. For while Boone is handier with a gun, he's mighty hot-headed. And Jeremy Lee's nerves is made outa steel. Man, but I must not miss that fight!"

And so, like some impartial spectator, Beaver Brown watched this dangerous game being played. And as Jawbone, fear driven, his whisky gone, crept from rock to bush, from coulee to coulee, half-starved, half-mad, the trapper counted the miles that he would have to make before he stumbled on to Boone's camp. Or before Tex Harmer, likewise afoot, would meet Jawbone.

Harmer, almost as ragged now as Jawbone in his shredded and soiled finery, was also working toward the Highwoods. But Harmer's way was not Jawbone's way. The Texan was cunning as a wolf, and his trail was the predatory trail of a wolf. He stole food from camps along the Shonkin. He was travelling afoot now by preference. Beaver had found his high-heeled boots discarded in a brush patch and the faint tracks away from that brush patch were made by moccasins. Tex Harmer was feeling his way to the safety that lay beyond the Shonkin range, where a man on horseback travelling alone might be the target for bullets of a sheriff's posse. Wherein showed the canny wisdom of the killer. When Tex Harmer died, he would die hard. Warned by the mysterious theft of the horse he had gained by murder, Tex Harmer would move with caution. Beaver never got within gun range of Harmer now, because the Texan was wily and dangerous. Tex Harmer would strike with the rapidity of a coiled rattler, only he would not warn before he struck.

"Boone," argued Beaver to himself, "can draw a faster gun than Tex Harmer. But he'll never get the chance to draw if Harmer has his say-so. He'll kill the boy without warnin'. There's times when I wish I'd dropped that varmint when the chance come my way. But that'd be interferin' with fate. Which brings a man bad luck. And I don't want to be crossin' no bad luck till I see ol' Jawbone get his.

Then I'll hole up with whisky and grub and live like a king, trappin' some, just to keep my hand in, drinkin' plenty, eatin' fresh meat, gettin' my livin' from the trap lines strung by the fools as works the north country for Hudson's Bay. Gettin' along about time for to be pushin' north'ards, too. Snow's due in a month or so. Time for ol' Beaver to be headin' north'ards. But I kain't go till I sees the finish here. Which ain't so far off, as I reads the sign."

Chapter 24

A Man of Quality

It was getting dusk that evening when Boone heard the sharp crackle of rifle fire, perhaps a mile down the creek. He saddled his horse and examined his Winchester. Hiding his horse in some dense brush, he took the gun and worked his way down toward where the shooting was going on. He had squatted in some buckbrush when a man on foot came up the creek. The man was like some hunted animal. Dodging, crawling, running. His breath was labored, his gait weary and desperate in its effort to make speed. He fell once crossing a clearing, there between the box-elder clumps. Now he fell once more, almost within arm's reach of Boone's hiding place. The man, ragged, bearded, mud-caked, lay there, trying to rise. Boone stepped from his shelter. The fugitive saw him, lifted his gun, then dropped the barrel, so that it did not cover the boy.

"It's me, Jawbone," called Boone cautiously. "Don't you know me, old top?"

"I know you, young un. Otherwise, I'd 'a' killed you. Get, quick! Get outa here! They're after me, blast 'em! They'll be here directly. Get out, boy!"

"Who's comin', Jawbone?" Boone dragged the tottering derelict into shelter. Something in Jawbone's manner swept away the boy's hatred for the man.

"I dunno, Boone I swear to Heaven, I dunno! I'm dyin', young un. They got me. Gimme some ca'tridges. I'll make a stand here. I'm bad hit. I'll go out a-fightin'. You're a good boy. Always was. I been ornery. Get away, boy, get plumb away! It ain't for you to stay here. Get out! Find Judge Lee. Tell him I sent you. Tell him Jawbone sent you to him. That I never meant to shoot him. I was loco drunk. Thought he was reachin' for a gun and plugged him. Like I done told the ghost of Beaver Brown. You're. . . . Boy, here they come!"

Boone pulled the stricken, wounded, mud-spattered man into the brush. Rifle bullets sprayed the willows now. Jawbone tried to pull the boy down, begging him to run. But something inside Boone would not let him quit this man, who was more beast than human, a hunted, dying thing smeared with red and mud.

Into Boone's mind and heart swept the memories of those days and nights when Jawbone had treated him with a pitiful sort of comradeship. He could not leave the man here to be shot down. Boone stood up, heedless of danger. He raised his hat above his head, waving it.

"Who are you?" he shouted. "What do you want? There's a man dying here. He's had a-plenty of your lead. For Heaven's sake, hold your fire!"

A lull now in the firing. Then a single shot ripped the silence, missing Boone's head by a scant inch. Tex Harmer's hard voice croaked a profane taunt. Boone dropped to the ground beside Jawbone.

"We'll give 'em bullet for bullet, pardner," he grimly told the man who was shoving cartridges into his rifle magazine.

Sheltered in the brush and granite rocks, Boone and Jawbone fought off the men who surrounded them. Through the rattle of gunfire sounded Tex Harmer's cold voice.

It was but yesterday that Harmer had been picked up by the men who had followed him along the outlaw trails. Jeremy Lee, riding as their leader, had sighted Tex Harmer travelling on foot. He had ridden alone to where Tex Harmer stood waiting with his hand on his gun.

"I supposed you were dead," the river gambler had said, without the formality of any other words of greeting.

"You supposed wrong, then." Harmer's voice matched the gambler's in coldness. "I'm alive, amigo. And I'm ready any time to settle up with the sneakin' coyote that set me afoot. You know what I'm talkin' about all right. I simply had to kill a man to get that horse."

Jeremy Lee's eyebrows lifted a trifle. "I supposed you were dead, Harmer. We found your dead horse in the river. And there's a sheriff's posse hunting the hills for Jawbone Smith on the supposition that he killed a cowboy to get the cowboy's horse. It seems they accuse brother Jawbone wrongly. I'm glad you told me that you did that cold-blooded job. And don't ever call me a sneaking coyote again, my friend. Don't ever call me any kind of a slurring name, because it will bring you some bad luck. Your hand is on your gun, brother Harmer; I'd like to lay you a bet that I could kill you before you can draw it."

"You're a tricky fellow," snarled Harmer. "I've seen you work. I'll pick my own time to kill you."

The other men came up. Jeremy Lee smiled thinly, never taking his eyes from Tex Harmer.

"Harmer," said the river gambler, "there can be only one leader in the wolf pack. I'll fight you for it, or I'll be willing to let our pack of rogues decide which of us shall lead them on to further crimes. Which will it be? Fight or vote?"

"Let the boys decide," said Tex Harmer. "Whoever they pick, goes with them. The other man pulls out, alone."

Tex Harmer's sinister face lighted up. He knew that they followed Jeremy Lee only for lack of a better leader. These human wolves did not trust this polished gambler, who often angered them with his contemptuous sarcasm. They feared and distrusted a man who had been born and reared among gentlefolk. Tex Harmer was their own kind. They could understand his talk and his ways.

"Well, thieves and cut-throats," said Jeremy Lee, "decide."

"We'll foller Tex Harmer," said one of them. "We was with him at Red Rock, and we'll stay with him here. You're kinda high-toned to be herdin' with us fellers that don't know how to eat with more than one fork. You've rawhided us and sneered at us and made us take it. You better ride on, Mister Tinhorn."

Either by chance or premeditation, Jeremy Lee had so maneuvered his horse that his back was to a clay-cut bank. He faced them now with lips that twisted with contempt and eyes that glittered with a killer's cruelty. The member of the outlaw band who had spoken so boldly was a heavy-faced giant, bearded, unwashed, half-drunk. The gambler's silence, mistaken for timidity, prompted the man to further words. He felt, perhaps, that Jeremy Lee would now take insults in the face of such odds.

"Ride on, tinhorn. Take your fancy words, and high-toned ways, and dude clothes, and drift yonderly. We got ol' Tex back. We'll foller him to the end."

"You will indeed, my unbathed *compadre,*" said Jeremy Lee. "For once in your life, you've unwittingly spoken the truth. Eternity's gates stand ajar waiting for your coming. You called me a tinhorn. I'm giving you about three seconds to say you lie. Say it or pull that gun, you —"

With a snarl, the man's gun slid into sight. Jeremy Lee's right hand moved in a short arc. Two spurts of red from the little derringer, and the big outlaw, with a choking oath, slid from his saddle, shot through the head.

Now a long-barrelled six-shooter filled each of the river gambler's hands. One gun covered Tex Harmer.

"Now, you pack of mongrels," said Jeremy Lee, "who takes up that fool's job of killing me? Make a move, any of you, and these guns begin talking. Tex Harmer will get the first bullet square in the heart. Around and 'round the little ball goes, and where it stops, nobody knows. Step up, gents, and place your bets."

The gambler's lips taunted them, mocked them, insulted them. His slitted black eyes held them with their glitter. No man dared move.

"You needed a horse and saddle, Harmer," he finished. "I've just given you one. Now get out of here, all of you. Ride on, you pack of mongrel-bred dogs! You chose to follow Tex Harmer. Follow him, then."

Tex Harmer dared not risk the chance of pulling his gun. His pocked face white and twisted, he mounted the horse from the back of which the river gambler had just shot a man. He rode away, his men following.

Jeremy Lee, his back to the clay-cut

bank, watched them ride away. The gambler's handsome face was mask-like. When they had gone, he dismounted and searched the pockets of the dead man. What he found, he wrapped in the dead man's silk neckscarf and stowed in his saddle pockets. Then he covered the dead man's face and rode away alone, erect in the saddle as a cavalry officer on parade.

So Tex Harmer came back into command of his renegade pack. And on the next day they had jumped Jawbone Smith, as that half-starved, half-mad outlaw was making his way on foot toward the Highwoods.

So Tex Harmer and his men now surrounded Boone and Jawbone. And from a brush-covered knoll, Beaver Brown watched the fight through a pair of army binoculars.

Beaver saw Tex Harmer throw his men in a circle around the spot where Boone and Jawbone fought grimly under the hissing, whining, snarling bullets that clipped the brush and spattered the sand rocks.

Now he saw a rider on a black horse coming swiftly out of the dusk. The rider swung out of the saddle and came on afoot, his rifle ready. He was passing up the creek within a stone's throw of where Beaver squatted. The trapper lifted his nasal voice.

"Come up here, Jeremy Lee."

The river gambler dropped from view behind some rocks. "Who are you?"

"Skeered ye, did I?" chuckled the trapper. "Who be I? That's a hard question. I'm no friend of Tex Harmer's, lay your coin on that bet. And I'm no friend of Jawbone's, for that matter. But there's twenty of them varmints to two. And Jawbone's hit bad. I was just about to whittle down them odds with my meat getter when you popped into sight, skylighted fair and purty. Come up here, young feller, and we'll augur out a campaign, soldier-like."

Something in the cracked voice allayed the gambler's fear of treachery. He climbed through the brush and rocks, to find the buckskin-clad trapper puffing an evil-smelling pipe, his long rifle across a rock, the field glasses in his bony hands.

"You been ridin' these hills for weeks, yet you turn up a-lookin' like a beaver hat just took out of a band box. That's quality, son. And it's ol' Beaver Brown as admires quality in a man. Squat lower, or you'll draw gunfire, mayhap. Light up your pipe."

Jeremy Lee smiled. Without a word, he

handed the trapper one of his long cheroots.

"If it is downright necessary to smoke," he told Beaver, "use a decent weed."

"And the pleasure, Jeremy Lee, belongs to me. I run out of plug and been smokin' kinnikinnick, which I borrows off of some Injun friends. And the stuff ain't to my likin'. I've been raised on good natural leaf terbaccer and corn likker as was aged in hickory wood. Bad 'baccy and bad likker is my lot now. And I kin add, bad company, save for the present company o' yourself, Jeremy Lee."

The river gambler chuckled. Here was a character who pleased his fancy. Between the two men, for all their difference in bearing, was a quickly made bond of understanding.

"You know me," said Jeremy Lee, when the trapper handed him the field glasses.

"Since you was knee-high to a prairie dog. I knowed your father. Fit under him in the war."

A quick look from the gambler. Beaver chuckled.

"He was killed," said Beaver, "in Mexico. I've stood by his grave down there."

"Then you know who —"

"I know nothin', Jeremy Lee, excep' that I keep my tongue from waggin', and I don't go askin' money from men to keep me from talkin'. I've got many a fault, Jeremy Lee, but blackmailin' ain't among 'em. I knowed your daddy, and once, down in Mexico, he saved my worthless hide. Down yonder in the brush with my ol' pard Jawbone is a lad they call Boone. Do you know who his daddy was?"

"Yes, I think I do."

"You come here, mayhap, to kill him?"

"No. Quite the contrary. I'll chance a few bullets to yank him out of this uneven fight. I'm after Tex Harmer."

"Supposin' the lad called Boone gets back to Fort Benton?"

"So much the better," replied the gambler. "That's where he belongs. He'll get fair play and what belongs to him."

"What about you?"

"I'll go back down the same river that I travelled up. But before I go, there's a debt or two to pay off with a gun."

"Meanin' who?"

"Meaning Tex Harmer for one, Jawbone Smith for the other. That will balance my books."

"And then you'll be a-goin' down the river again?"

"There will be no other alternative after Boone returns to Fort Benton."

"But if Boone was to get killed, what then, Jeremy Lee?"

"I might stay."

"Dependin', mayhap," said Beaver, a sly twinkle in his fox-like eyes, "on what a certain young lady had to say?"

"Perhaps," said the river gambler softly, "you're right. But if we can kill off Harmer, the others of his scurvy band will run. And Boone will be saved from being killed or having to kill Tex Harmer. Even if Boone killed Tex Harmer — which he most surely will if ever he gets to line his sights on the blackguard — that killing will mar something very wonderful in his life and the life of a certain young lady."

"This here young lady don't fancy killin's?"

"Because the judge's sorrow over a tragic duel he once fought, and his own recent shooting has put a horror of guns and bloodshed in her heart."

"And while this here young lady is almighty fond of Boone, she'd mayhap lose that fondness if he turned out to be a killer?"

"That's the point. And I think we'd

better be taking a hand in yonder battle before it's too late."

"Aye, Jeremy Lee. And for all as may be said against you, I'll say you're a brave man and a good loser if ever I see one. It takes quality in a man to do as you're doin'. Let's get goin'!"

Chapter 25

"So Long, Pardner"

As best he could, Boone tied up Jawbone's wounds. The renegade thanked him. Indeed, it was one of the few thanks Jawbone had ever given the boy.

That circle of gunfire was closing tighter on the two trapped fighters. An hour yet until darkness, and Harmer would try to finish them before then so as to prevent them from slipping away in the gloom. Boone kept trying to sight Tex Harmer.

"Oncet we get him," Jawbone had gritted, "his pack of coyotes will travel on. There's a sheriff's posse been ridin' the hills, and this shootin' may draw 'em. Which ain't to Tex Harmer's likin', for he's yaller plumb down his back. I'd like for to ketch sight of him while I'm still able to draw a steady bead. Ain't got long to live, and I'd like just one. . . . Listen!"

Above the din of rifle fire sounded a wild, plainsman's yell. Indian-like in its high-pitched ferocity. Jawbone's eyes grew wide with fear.

"You heard that yell, young un? It's ol' Beaver Brown's ghost as has been a-follerin' me, drivin' me mad. It's Beaver's war whoop. Hear it?"

"Plenty plain, Jawbone. But it's no ghost. Beaver is alive."

"Don't you ever think that. Beaver's dead. I killed him twenty years ago, in New Mexico. He drove me to it with his eternal gabblin' and cacklin'. And that's him as waits for me yon side of the black river. It's my judgment a-comin'! I'm a-dyin' and ol' Beaver'll be waitin' for me. He's trailed me for weeks, I tell you, knowin' my time to die was a-comin'. It's my dues, for I done murder. Black murder it was, young un, and it's black murder as is charged to me on the Big Book . . . Hear the ol' varmint yell!"

Beaver was doing more than yelling. From rock to brush patch, his gun spewing fire, his lanky frame twisting and dodging grotesquely, he came leaping.

His wild war cry had something of that coyote cry that multiplies in volume until one would wager a dozen of the animals were yelping. There was a terrifying blood-thirstiness to its savage notes that made

Boone shiver. Now, Tex Harmer's men, suddenly grown panicky when they learned this new danger that menaced, and deceived by Beaver's multiple-sounding yells, took to their horses. Tex Harmer, cursing them, shouted futile orders, then was forced to follow them in their flight.

He spurred his horse to a run. Just as Jeremy Lee, mounted on his powerful black, met him face to face. Their guns roared at almost the same instant. Red stained the river gambler's cheek. Tex Harmer lurched in his saddle, his pocked face twisted, his gun dropping from a hand that hung useless, the arm smashed at the wrist. As his left hand went for his second gun, the river gambler, cool as a man at target practice, shot again. Tex Harmer's twisted mouth was snarling. His left arm was smashed below the shoulder. Helpless, he could not even guide his unruly horse. He lost his balance and was thrown into some bushes. Jeremy Lee was out of the saddle and on the ground, tying the outlaw's legs.

"I'll be back directly, my amigo," he told the snarling prisoner. "I've not intention of letting you die of your wounds. You're slated to stretch rope."

Jeremy Lee and Beaver met. Together

they rode toward the rocks where Boone stood, his rifle in his hands. His gray, black-flecked eyes were hard, suspicious, as he recognized Jeremy Lee.

"I just saw you down Tex Harmer," he said to the river gambler. "What is it you want of me? If it's to go back to Fort Benton, that's where I'm goin', but I'm goin' alone."

"That," said Jeremy Lee, "is your privilege, so far as I'm concerned. Myself, I'm not returning there, so will you hand Tex Harmer over to the authorities? Where is Jawbone Smith?"

"Jawbone," said Boone simply, "has gone. He's crossed the Big Divide. I'll take care of his body."

"That is as it should be."

"You treated me a might shabby, there at Fort Benton," said Boone, "but you and Beaver have just saved my life. A man can't discount that. I'm thankin' you both."

"My friend," said Jeremy Lee, "when you return to Fort Benton, there will be no charges for you to face. Lieutenant Clanton has, by this time, departed for another climate, and will have resigned from the army. The horse you left at Judge Lee's ranch will be your property. I've learned he was stolen from the army post by Tex

Harmer. Jawbone, in turn, stole that horse and another one from Harmer. So that settles that case.

"Concerning the Red Rock bank robbery, Tex Harmer engineered that and threw the blame elsewhere to shield himself. He'll hang. You're cleared of that charge.

"Regarding the shooting of Judge Lee, I can say only this to defend myself against the bad treatment accorded you. The night of our afternoon's meeting at the river, I set out to gamble. I happened to overhear Jawbone Smith and a man named Pete discussing the shooting of one 'Big Nose,' who had been set to watch you. Also, they mentioned a well-laid plot to blackmail Judge Lee. They were to use you as the proverbial monkey, as it were, to drag the chestnuts from the fire. I had no way of knowing, just then, how deeply you were involved in the plot. That dying man had spoken to you, mentioning one Tex Harmer, whom I knew to be a killer and an all-around blackguard.

"I listened carefully, and I made my plans. To save Judge Lee, I would stay in Fort Benton. He had taken me, an orphan, and raised me. Educated me. Saw me turn from decency to a gambler who lived by his wits. I saw a chance to return, perhaps, a little of the generosity, tolerance, and understanding Judge Lee had shown me. I knew that there was a hidden chapter in his life that concerned the duel he fought with Frank Boone, a Kentuckian. And to guard him from harm, I stayed in Fort Benton to wipe out the men who sought Judge Lee's ruin. My job is done. What I have done, be it right or wrong, I have done to save the honor of one of the finest men who ever lived. When I thought you were against him, I was against you. When I learned that you were innocent, wholly ignorant of the plot that so involved you, I was glad to help you as well as Judge Lee.

"In Fort Benton, Judge Lee is waiting to see you. A friend of yours named Till Driscoll has left a letter for you with the sheriff. Get it and read it before you go to see Judge Lee. And now, my friend, I'll be going my way. Beaver will help you with Tex Harmer and Jawbone's body."

The river gambler smiled. "I'm going down the river. I don't reckon that our trails will ever again cross. I would like to shake hands in farewell. I would like to wish you happiness in the new life that is opening for you."

"And I wish you luck," said Boone,

moved by the gambler's manner. They silently gripped hands. Jeremy Lee shook hands with Beaver, then rode away into the gathering darkness.

"Fate," chuckled the trapper. "Trails cross in mighty queer places. Let's pick a good spot to plant our ol' pard Jawbone. Then we'll move on to town with Tex Harmer. Take a look at his hurts, laddie, while ol' Beaver rides to his camp for a shovel. I'll be back by moonshine, and we'll plant ol' Jawbone deep with a nice granite rock for a headstone. He went out with his boots on and his gun a-smokin', did ol' Jawbone. A-thinkin' ol' Beaver was waitin' for him where he's gone."

Beaver Brown rode away, chuckling and muttering. Boone bandaged Tex Harmer's two wounds and held a hatful of water to the suffering man's lips. The killer did not even trouble to thank Boone.

When Beaver returned with the shovel, the moon was up. Boone and the trapper dug a deep grave and buried Jawbone. While Beaver started for Fort Benton with the prisoner, Boone lingered at this unmarked grave.

Bareheaded, he stood there. He owed little to the dead renegade. Yet, now that the man was dead, loneliness crept into the heart of the boy, who was nineteen before he knew that the renegade outlaw was not his father. Now, Jawbone was dead. In Fort Benton there awaited him some message. Boone knew now that, in some manner, his future lay with Judge Lee. There, in this historic town at the head of navigation on the Missouri River, lay the solving of the mystery that shrouded Boone's parentage. Judge Lee had killed a man named Boone in a duel. Perhaps that man had been his father. Eager to get this puzzle solved, Boone would be leaving this fresh grave in a few minutes.

"God," he spoke softly to the stars, "some ways, Jawbone was good to me. The whisky done it. I reckon you'll kinda understand how he wasn't responsible. So far as I'm concerned, there's nothin' to say against Jawbone."

Boone laid a hand on the granite rock that marked the new grave.

"So long, Jawbone, old pardner. Rest quiet."

Chapter 26

Good-bye, Guns

At Fort Benton, Boone turned over Tex Harmer to the sheriff. Beaver Brown had quit Boone before they crossed the river.

"Yonder, among quality folks, laddie," Beaver had said, "lies your trail. Mine goes on. You'll be seein' me no more, for I'm stayin' clear of you and yourn. Tell Judge Lee that Beaver Brown, him as he met on the Miles City stage road that day, holds no bad will agin' him. That I never did. And that I was not mixed up in the blackmail plot with Fouchet, Jawbone, and the others. They're dead now, the pack of 'em. Jawbone went last, which was fittin' an' proper, as he was the toughest of the lot. So long, laddie, and good luck."

The sheriff greeted Boone warmly. "Knew you'd come back, once I figgered out why you quit jail. Well, them SL boys has the wrinkles took outa their stomachs now, I bet." He chuckled and spun the combination of his safe.

"Here's a letter from Till Driscoll. Sit here and read it. I'll be gone for a while."

Boone took the letter. His eyes met those of the sheriff. The older man puffed hard at his cigar.

"Somethin' kinda tells me, sheriff," said Boone, "that what is in this letter is gonna make Judge Lee and his daughter almighty sad. From what I've picked up, here and there, I'm kinda connected with a man named Boone who was killed by Judge Lee."

"Frank Boone," said the sheriff, "was your father. Lee killed him in a fair duel. Lee was in the hospital for a long time. Frank Boone lived a week. Durin' that week, while he lived, he made his will. He settled up his affairs and died, leavin' an only son, whose mother was dead. That son was a little codger, christened Daniel in honor of the old scout who, while probably no kin, was a man good enough to name a boy for. You are that Daniel Boone."

"That," said Boone, "is all that I need to know, I reckon."

There was a fire going in the stove, for the morning was a chilly one. Before the sheriff could stop him, Boone tossed the unopened bulky envelope into the fire. He

227

smiled at the sheriff, an odd look in his flecked eyes.

"That finishes that, sir."

"Hang me for a hoss thief, young man, if you ain't a queer un! I wonder if you know what's burnin' up there in that stove?"

"No, sir, not exactly. I only know that it's burnin' somethin' for keeps that's better for its bein' buried." He held out his hand to the law officer.

"I'll be a-driftin' along, I reckon."

"Where do you aim to go, boy?"

"I don't know. Just along the trail, I reckon."

"Judge Lee and his daughter want to see you. It wouldn't be fair not to see him, son. Will you go?"

"If he wants it that a way, and you think I should go see him, I'll go."

Boone got on his horse and rode to the Lee home, to which the injured man had been moved. It was a tall brick house, with cupolas, and a large lawn shaded by big cottonwoods. Even as Boone stepped off his horse, Virginia Lee came down the walk to the gate. At the sight of Boone she halted. Then, with a glad cry, she came running.

"My father's prayers and mine are answered," she said, tears in her eyes.

"You've come back to us. And you'll stay." She took both his hands in hers, dragging him along the walk.

Boone, embarrassed, his emotions whirling, let himself be thus led up the steps and on to the veranda where the judge sat in a big chair propped with pillows. The judge's face worked with emotion, and his handsome, kindly eyes spoke volumes as he gripped Boone's hand, and Virginia pushed a chair toward the embarrassed cowboy.

"God has been kind in returning you to us, son. You understand that this is now your home. That what is mine is likewise yours. But it is something other than material things that I will try to give you. Through my fault your boyhood years have been worse than wasted. You know the story by now, of course?"

"I know that Frank Boone was my father, sir. The letter at the sheriff's office I burned without openin'."

"Why, sir?" asked the judge, smiling.

"Because I reckoned what was in it would hurt you and Miss Virginia, and I reckoned you'd suffered a-plenty."

"And you were going away, I'll bet, without seeing us? Am I right?" asked Virginia.

"I figgered that was the best thing to do. The sheriff showed me I was wrong. So here I am. But I won't bother you, sir. I reckon that bringin' up old memories like it does, seein' me, won't help make you-all happy. And I'm just a cowboy with no book learnin' or manners."

Judge Lee gripped Boone's arm. "Hear what I have to say, my boy. Then, if you wish, I'll let you go."

Virginia pulled up a chair near Boone's. The judge smiled at the boy and girl, his eyes a little misty.

"Frank Boone was my friend," the judge began, "and we had been friends a long time, when politics, and the war, and a complication of things, pushed that friendship apart and salted the wound of its severing with a foolish enmity. That enmity was not of Frank's doing, nor of mine. My adopted brother, Jeremy, was the cause of it. He had always hated Frank Boone. And Jeremy was cruel, clever and vindictive. He was much like his son, whom you've met. He hid his good side under a cold exterior. He was a gambler and a border buccaneer. It was Jeremy who forced the duel on Frank and me. We were both hot-tempered, quick to resent an insult.

"We met. We fought. You know the result. I lived, but Frank died. Before he died, he made his will. That will left everything to his son Daniel, a mere baby who, being motherless, was being cared for at a friend's home. The last will and testament drawn up left Frank Boone's estate to his son. And, oddly enough, I was made sole guardian and trustee. Frank trusted me. And, knowing that he was going to die, he realized his folly and mine. And he knew that, if the boy were given into my charge, I would do all in my power to care for the child. I was to rear Daniel as my own son, understand, and give him a home, and love, and all that makes for a boy's happiness and future success as a man.

"I was so badly hurt that it was many weeks before I learned of Frank's death and this last will he had made. When the will was read to me, I made all arrangements to take Frank Boone's son into my home. Virginia was not yet born, and my wife and I were anxious to take Frank's son as our own.

"I sent for the child, only to learn that Frank Boone's son had died. My foster brother, Jeremy, gave me the details of the child's death. I believed him. The duel had wrecked my health and happiness. I was a broken man. Broken in health and in hopes. Knowing that Frank forgave me was all that kept me from taking my own life. At the advice of my friends, I left the South and came here to Fort Benton. The courage and loyalty of my wife were things to make any man believe in God and the Mother of God.

"Now came a letter from Mexico, telling me of my foster brother Jeremy's death. He was killed somewhere down there. Before he died, he mailed a letter to me. In this letter he begged my forgiveness for his misdeeds. And he informed me that Frank Boone, before he fought the duel, had made out a statement to be given his son in case he was shot to death. This statement was a farewell letter to his son. In that letter he commanded that son to avenge his father's death. The son should be trained in the use of guns, then he should hunt me down and kill me."

The judge's grip on the boy's arm tightened. Boone saw the old grief line the man's face.

"My father left me such a letter, sir?"

"It was among the letters Jawbone carried. But Frank Boone, perhaps, never composed it. I've now begun to wonder if it was not a forgery. But to get back to Jeremy's last letter. It told me that Frank

Boone's son was not dead, but alive, and was being cared for by a man who had been Frank's orderly in the war. This man, one of Quantrell's raiders, now turned outlaw, had Frank's son, and was rearing the boy to be a killer. So that, if I did not pay ransom to this man and his cronies, they would hold the boy in readiness to shoot me down.

"That was the first information concerning the living boy who was Frank Boone's son. Then, after my foster brother's death, other letters came. Sinister letters, telling me of the boy's marksmanship, his temper when angry, his adaptability to the evil companionship that was now his lot. And always the writer hinted that some day he would come to collect what belonged to the boy under the threat of that boy's guns.

"I'd sent for Jeremy's son after his father's death. I educated him and gave him a home. But I began to mistrust him. I have never been able to understand him. And when he asked my permission to pay court to my daughter, I refused him flatly. He was so angry I feared he would attack me. He left my roof and became a river gambler and Heaven knows what else.

"Then I got a letter from him. A strange

letter. It stated that he knew the band of outlaws who were threatening me. And that if I would let him pay court to Virginia, he would locate Frank Boone's son for me and would put an end to this blackmail band.

"In desperation, I replied, telling him to come to Fort Benton and talk this over with me. Those letters were becoming more frequent, more bold in their threats. They taunted me with the fact that I had invested Frank Boone's money in this ranch on the Teton. That I had misused funds belonging to this young man who was coming to call for his accounting. Coming with a gun.

"The rest," said Judge Lee, "you know — how that Jawbone fellow attacked me, of Jeremy's part, all of it. Now it is settled. And if you would like to bring happiness into the heart of a man whose burden of grief has been hard to bear, you will make your home with us. The ranch belongs to you. The Hanleys, you will find, are the best on earth. Virginia has helped me pray that you would come back to us for always. You'll grant our prayers, son?"

Boone tried to speak, but his voice choked in his throat. With an odd smile, he unbuckled his gun belt and handed it to the girl.

"I wonder," he said, his voice shaking, "if I could swap this for a few books?"

Virginia nodded, her eyes misty. With a quick little sob, she was in his arms. The judge, his face radiant, slipped from his chair and tiptoed into the house.

And so Boone, the drifting cowboy, found the end of his trial.